BECOMING BULLY PROOF

RICH GROGAN
Master Martial Arts Instructor

Becoming Bully Proof
Published by AME High Publishing, LLC
Palmetto, FL

ISBN: 978-0-9988490-2-7
JUVENILE FICTION / Social Themes / Bullying

Publisher's Cataloging-in-Publication data

Names: Grogan, Rich, author.
Title: Becoming bully proof / Rich Grogan.
Description: Palmetto, FL: AME High Publishing LLC, 2022. | Summary: Twelve-year-old Logan is a quiet, big-hearted middle school kid who just wants to fit in but his kind heart is a magnet for bullies.
Identifiers: ISBN: 978-0-9988490-2-7
Subjects: LCSH Bullying--Juvenile fiction. | Interpersonal relations--Juvenile fiction. | Middle schools--Fiction. | Martial arts--Juvenile fiction. | BISAC JUVENILE FICTION / Social Themes / Bullying
Classification: LCC PZ7.1 .G758 2022 | DDC [Fic]--dc23

Cover and Interior Design by Victoria Wolf at wolfdesignandmarketing.com.

QUANTITY PURCHASES: Schools, companies, professional groups, clubs, and other organizations may qualify for special terms when ordering quantities of this title. For information, email rg@warriorconfidence.com.

PRAISE FOR
BECOMING BULLY PROOF

"Read this book and be empowered today with the hope & self-confidence to believe in yourself to make a difference in your life and the lives of your children- but only if you stand up to the bully and take action!"

—Tom Ziglar, CEO *of Zig Ziglar Corporations*, and proud son of legendary master motivator, Zig Ziglar.

"Becoming Bully Proof is a rare gem … Authentic and real-world, it's packed full of powerful lessons on dealing with adversity and building resilience that every parent and child should read."

—Lt Col Waldo Waldman, author of the New York Times and Wall Street Journal Bestseller *Never Fly Solo*.

Dedicated to anyone who has experienced the emotional, psychological, and physical pain of being bullied. To those who lost the struggle because they felt there was no hope, and to those now fighting to overcome this pain.

You are not alone, and there is always hope.

ACKNOWLEDGMENTS

FIRST AND FOREMOST, I thank God for all my blessings.

To my amazingly supportive wife, Desi, who has been my pillar of strength for over thirty years and has never lost hope or given up on me, even though I gave her every reason to do so.

To my awesome kids, Austin, Madelyn, and Emmitt, whose patience and understanding are what made this book possible. I am eternally grateful for all the love and support you give me each and every day, as I work to become the best father I can be.

To my mom, dad, and sister for helping me establish the work ethic I have today, from all the hard work and countless lessons growing up on the farm.

To my Grandma Bonnie for all her love, Bible scriptures, and not-so-subtle reminders. "Richy, are you putting God first?" "Richy, what's your integrity worth?"

To my mentors, coaches, and instructors: Sa Bom Nim George Manns, Hanshi Dave Kovar, Master Chip Townsend, Professor Brannon Beliso, Chris Widener, and Tom Ziglar.

A HUGE thank you doesn't even come close to saying how grateful I am for all your love, support, belief, and guidance throughout this project and my life.

I am blessed beyond words. God bless each and every one of you.

FOREWORD

I'LL NEVER FORGET STANDING in the public school health check line, waiting to be checked for lice, when I was thirteen. It was humiliating, for sure. The class bully was standing behind me, and I clearly remember thinking, "Be small. ... Don't attract attention. ..." Consequently, he was looking for someone to harass, and I seemed to be the easiest target. Sounds about right ...

Having lost an eye when I was three years old, donning an awkward-fitting prosthesis didn't help my case against the bully. My prosthetic eye was big and didn't move like my other eye. To top it off, my nickname is "Chip." Living in Texas, there were plenty of ways to poke at the name "Chip"—chocolate-Chip, cow-Chip—you get the point. It was hard for me to blend in.

While I was anxiously waiting, hoping, that this bully would leave me alone, the prodding started. Most days, I could ignore his words, but on this day, he sneered, "Townsend, I'm going to poke out your other eye!"

It occurred to me right then and there that I had no idea what I would do if he tried. And that thought absolutely terrified me. That's the day I told my mom that I wanted to start martial arts. That's the day that altered the course of my life forever.

Soon after, I started a journey that showed me I could get up whenever I fell and stand tall in the face of adversity, and it helped me understand my strengths. This caused a shift in me. I wasn't the scrawny, easy-to-pick-on "disabled" kid anymore. I was someone who carried myself with confidence and knew how to navigate challenges. The "target" on my back had moved, and martial arts is what moved it. I went from the victim to the one who would stand up for others. The confidence I gained allowed me to hold my head high and carry myself in a way that was a deterrent to anyone seeking easy prey.

Rich Grogan's tale about Logan and how he faces bullies will give you another way to look at being Bully Proof. As I reflect on this stellar story, one of my favorite parenting quotes comes to mind:

"It's not what you do for your children, but what you have taught them to do for themselves, that makes them successful human beings." – Ann Landers

It is my hope that the readers of this story are empowered to equip EVERYONE with the tools to be BULLY PROOF.

– Chip Townsend
14x ISKA (International Sport Karate Association) Breaking World Champion 6th Degree Black Belt; Owner, Team Chip Martial Arts Centers; chiptownsend.com

CHAPTER 1

JOE SPRANG UP IN BED YELLING "DON'T TOUCH ME!" Sweating, with fists clenched and a racing heart, Joe had so much adrenaline pumping through his veins that he could've punched a hole through the wall. It was 2:00 a.m., and he was all alone and completely safe in his own house. He looked around the bedroom with the intensity of a tiger ready to pounce, but nothing was there, just the images in his head.

In his nightmare, he was twelve years old again, and Bob and Mike, two of the meanest bullies in school, had him trapped in the locker room.

They had cornered him between the lockers and the benches, just like they'd done many times before.

They started with name-calling and taunting, then took turns shoving him into the lockers over and over.

Joe wished that he had tried to run, or at least not gotten trapped in the corner, but he froze, as he always did at the sound of their voices.

They had been bullying him for years, and since he never did anything to stop it, it kept getting worse.

He wished he knew what to do or that someone would step in and help him, but those things never happened, and they weren't going to happen today either. He knew it, everyone standing around knew it, and worst of all, Bob and Mike knew it.

"Where do you think you're going?" Bob asked in a furious voice as Joe tried to crawl out of Bob's reach.

"He probably thinks we wouldn't find out about him crying to coach," Mike said as he got right up in Joe's face.

"Look at me when I'm talking to you!" Bob yelled, spitting with every word. He was only inches away from Joe's face.

"Yeah, show some respect!" Mike said as he slammed Joe's head against the lockers.

"You like that, baby Joe?!" Mike said, slamming Joe into the lockers again.

Joe put up his hands to try and protect himself, and when he did, Bob used the opening to knee Joe directly in the groin.

Joe let out a moan and fell to the floor, holding his groin. A group of boys had gathered around, but no one dared to say anything. Sure, everyone felt bad for Joe, but not bad enough to risk having it done to them, so they stood watching Joe curled up on the floor, wishing someone would help him. It was a case of, "Yeah, we feel sorry for you, but better you than me."

As Joe lay on the floor defenseless, Bob and Mike each reared back and kicked him several times in the stomach. And then to really prove their toughness, they each spit a big ball of snot into Joe's hair.

"Everyone see this?" Mike yelled out. "If you don't want this to happen to you, then you better stay out of our way."

"Yeah, and if any of you tells coach ... you're gonna get it worse!" Bob said, making sure to remind everyone that they were in charge.

That had happened over forty years ago, but after speaking with his sister, Molly, earlier in the day and discovering that the same thing was now happening to his nephew, those memories came flooding back, causing the nightmarish dream. But one thing was for sure: Joe wasn't going to let his nephew experience years of pain the way he had. Joe now knew the secrets to defeat bullying, and he was going to make sure his nephew, Logan, did too.

CHAPTER 2

"MOM, DO I REALLY HAVE TO GO to school today?" Logan asked, knowing the answer before the words ever left his lips.

"Yes, you're going to school. Now get your butt up, or you're going to be late," Molly replied.

"Mom, I can't find anything to wear, and I can't find any socks either."

"Just grab two socks ... they don't have to match ... we have to get going, or we'll be late again!".

Minutes later, Logan came rushing down the stairs wearing two mismatched socks, a pair of jeans, and an old red shirt.

Okay ... not what I would've picked, but at least he's dressed, his mom thought to herself. Logan rushed to get his shoes on and gulped down several bites of soggy cereal.

With cereal dripping from his chin, he grabbed his backpack and headed out to the car.

"How'd you sleep last night?" his mom asked as she put the car in drive.

"Okay, I guess," Logan answered without looking up.

"How are you feeling today? Are you excited about hockey practice tonight?"

"Yeah, I guess," Logan replied halfheartedly.

Sensing his lack of excitement, she asked, "What's wrong, Logan? Are you having trouble on the team?"

Logan just sat there quietly with his head down, then weakly said, "I sure miss Dad."

"I miss him too," she said in a sad tone as she got in the turn lane in front of Logan's school.

"Maybe I should just quit ... no one likes me anyway," Logan mumbled, barely loud enough for her to hear.

"Logan, that's not true," she said as she pulled up in front of the school and looked over at him.

Logan slowly unbuckled his seat belt and opened the door.

"Let's talk tonight after practice," his mom said as Logan got out of the car.

"Okay, Mom," Logan replied as he walked toward the school.

Logan's father had passed away a year earlier, and things were different now. His hero, who meant the world to him, was gone. The two of them had loved playing sports together, especially ice hockey. These days, Logan cried a lot and he had a hard time sleeping at night, so he had a hard time focusing at school. He was falling further and further behind in his homework, and to make matters worse, a couple of boys had started bullying him again. It started off with just name-calling and then laughing at him, but before long, as it always does, things started getting physical. The boys began shoving him and then hitting and kicking him in the locker room. Logan never did anything to defend himself, and no one else stepped in, so it just continued to get worse. He felt completely alone. He couldn't understand why this was happening and why no one at school ever helped him.

Logan was kindhearted, smart, and very well-mannered. He had blond hair and brown eyes and was small for his age, but due to the many chores and responsibilities he had growing up on a farm, he was very strong and muscular for his size. On the farm, Logan had to care for the horses and cows, which meant carrying heavy hay bales, filling up their water trough, and shoveling manure out of the stalls. He also took care of his two dogs and a new litter of kittens that lived in the barn.

Several months after his dad passed away, his mom, Molly, started home-schooling Logan. She thought this would give them a chance to work through the pain they were both feeling from the loss of his father, and it would help Logan get away from the daily bullying that was happening at school.

Things went as well as they could for the rest of that school year. Logan got caught up on all of his schoolwork, and as his self-esteem and self-confidence returned, so did his passion for playing hockey. Logan wanted to play on the school hockey team, and he knew that to play on the team, he would have to go back to school. So Logan was back in public school, and his mom returned to her full-time nursing career.

They were both nervous and knew it would be challenging, but Molly was hopeful that getting Logan back in school and playing hockey again would help him move forward.

That was the plan, anyway, and for the first several months, everything seemed to be moving along fine. Then

Logan started spending more time in his room, giving his mom attitude, and being disrespectful. He also started putting up a bigger fight about going to school.

Molly tried to convince herself that these were probably just normal teenage boy behaviors, and it was nothing more than a kid who didn't want to get up at 6:30 in the morning, but something told her that it was more. She had planned to talk with Logan when they both had some time, but right now wasn't that time, as they were already late.

Molly watched Logan slowly walk into the school. It was sad to see him this way, and her eyes welled with tears as she pulled out of the parking lot on her way to work.

As 3:30 p.m. rolled around, the time school was getting out, she sent Logan a text: "Hope you had a great day. Remember to get something to eat and get your homework done and I'll see you after practice. I love you."

She waited in anticipation for the reply. Five minutes went by, nothing, then ten minutes, still nothing, and she began to worry.

Maybe his phone was turned off, or maybe the battery was dead, or maybe he lost it, maybe, maybe, maybe. "Maybe I should just quit." The words echoed in her mind. Were these little clues that something was really wrong? Every time she started feeling this way, her mind would wander back to when Logan was in the third grade and she got called to come pick him up at school because of fighting.

She remembered how nervous she was driving to the school, and then how sad it was to see Logan sitting outside the principal's office, holding an ice pack to his bloody lip.

Logan had explained that two boys were continuously pushing him to the ground.

He tried over and over to get back up, but each time, he was shoved harder and harder back to the ground. Finally, he just gave up and lay there crying as a group of kids stood around laughing.

His friend, Tracey, tried to help him. She yelled at the two boys to leave him alone, and then yelled at everyone else, "SHUT UP and QUIT LAUGHING!"

But when she bent over to help Logan up, one of the boys pushed her on top of Logan, saying, "Why don't you kiss your boyfriend." Tracey fell hard to the ground, and her head hit Logan square in the face, causing his nose and top lip to start bleeding.

The boys ran away laughing as the other kids followed, leaving Logan and Tracey lying on the ground, crying and bleeding.

After getting an ice pack from the nurse and telling their story to the principal, they had a seat outside the office.

The two boys responsible were called to the office, and as they passed by Logan, one of the boys mumbled, "You're really going to get it now."

"Yeah, you're dead!" the other boy said as Logan sat there in fear.

The principal had talked to all the kids individually. He told them the school policy was that if two or more kids are involved in a physical confrontation, they are all equally guilty for not doing their part to avoid it.

Molly remembered how furious she was with the principal, and how upset she was that none of the school faculty did anything to help her son, even after he had repeatedly told them that he had been bullied for weeks. Now, here sat Logan with a bloody nose, a fat lip, and scratches all over his face, and he received the same punishment as the boys who did this to him. Tracey's parents were angry, too, because Tracey also got in trouble for being in the middle of the altercation.

Tracey's dad wanted to know how this policy made any sense. "How is it that my daughter," he demanded, "who was trying to do the right thing and help someone who was being bullied, ended up receiving the same punishment as the bullies?"

The principal said that Tracey may have had the right intentions, but the rule said that anyone involved in a conflict with another student is in violation of the school's "no tolerance" bullying policy.

Tracey's parents were so frustrated that they ended up pulling Tracey out of the school, which made things even tougher on Logan because now his one real friend was no longer at the school.

Logan was even more afraid than before. Not only did he get hurt, but he also got in trouble just for being involved. From then on, whenever anyone bullied him, he just took it and never tried to defend himself because he was more afraid of getting in trouble than he was of getting hurt.

As the bullying continued, it got to the point where Logan got physically sick and vomited nearly every day before school. He spent a great deal of time in the nurse's office with stomach pains caused by fear, stress, and the anxiety of possibly doing the wrong thing and getting in trouble.

Suddenly, her thoughts were interrupted by a text from Logan.

LOVE YOU TOO MOMMY!

"Mommy?" she asked herself. "When's the last time Logan called me 'Mommy?'"

She typed back: "Logan is that you? Is everything okay?"

"Everything's fine Mom, just heading to hockey practice," came the quick response.

She relaxed a bit and thought to herself that it was probably just boys giving Logan a hard time about his mom texting him.

She convinced herself that everything was okay until that evening when she saw Logan after practice. She tried to shake off the feeling that something wasn't right, but it was written all over Logan's face. As they walked to the car, it started raining, and she called out, "Come on, Logan, hurry up, you're getting soaked." But Logan didn't change his pace. By the time he got in the car, he was soaking wet and water was dripping off him as he sat there with his head down.

"What's wrong, Logan?"

Logan didn't reply, and he just sat there looking down.

"I can tell something's wrong. Didn't you have a good practice?"

"No, Mom, I didn't," Logan said flatly.

"Are you hurt, or did you just have a bad practice?"

"No, it's not that either. ... I just don't want to talk about it."

As they sat there quietly with only the sound of the radio in the background, Molly remembered when the two of them would rock out to the radio. They would turn it up and sing along with every song, but now things were different. Logan didn't seem to care what song was playing on the radio. He didn't seem to care much about anything.

Her thoughts were interrupted as she pulled to a stop in the driveway and Logan quickly hopped out of the car and ran upstairs to his room.

"Be sure to get a shower and then come downstairs for dinner," she yelled up the stairs.

"Mom, I just want to go to bed!"

"Logan, you need a shower, and you need to eat something."

"But Mom, I'm not hungry, and I just want to go to bed."

Several minutes passed, and when she didn't hear the water running, she headed upstairs to check on him.

"Logan, are you okay?" she asked, knocking softly on his door. "Please open the door."

Logan slowly opened the door, and she could see the tears on his face.

"Logan, what's going on?"

"Mom, I'm just tired and don't feel well."

She walked in and sat on the edge of his bed, patting the spot next to her for Logan to sit down. "Well, it's probably because you're hungry. You've been at school all day, then hockey practice, plus it's cold and raining out."

"Yeah, that's probably it," Logan replied.

"I want you to eat something."

"I'm really not hungry, Mom."

"Are you sick? Does your stomach hurt?"

"It hurts a little."

"What did you have for lunch today?"

Logan just shook his head as if to say nothing.

"Tell me what's going on, Logan," she insisted.

Without looking up, he said, "It's Doug and David again."

"What are they doing now?" she asked angrily.

"The same thing they've always done ... I just want to quit hockey and quit school."

"But Logan, you love playing hockey."

"I don't care anymore, Mom. I'm just done with it all, and I don't want to ever see those two again."

Logan began to cry harder as his mother put her arms around him. With tears streaming down his face, Logan told his mom about some of the horrible things Doug and David were doing to him. He told her about the time Doug knocked him on the floor and held him there while David rubbed his sweaty jockstrap in Logan's face, and the time the two of them took turns spitting on him. And another time when they repeatedly smacked him on his bare stomach until it was burning red, and how several times they threw his hockey equipment and his clothes in the shower with the water running.

She started crying along with Logan. "I am so sorry, Logan. Why didn't you ever tell me any of this?"

"Because I knew you would worry, and I thought I could deal with it ... and because I didn't want to quit hockey. But now it doesn't matter anymore. I just want to quit, and I want it all to go away."

"I'm so sorry, Logan."

"It's not your fault, Mom, but can I just quit?"

Before she could answer, Logan's cell phone began dinging with alerts. At first, it was just one, then another, then another, and in a matter of seconds, Logan's cell phone was blowing up with text messages.

"Logan, who's texting you?"

"I don't know, Mom, I usually ignore it."

"It must be pretty important; you've gotten about ten texts in the past thirty seconds."

"I don't care, Mom. I just want to go to bed."

"Okay, Logan, but first I want you to eat something."

Logan nodded his head in agreement and said he would be right down.

CHAPTER 3

WHILE FIXING LOGAN A BOWL of his favorite chicken noodle soup, Molly replayed their conversation in her head. She suddenly remembered something she had seen on the internet. It was a picture of a thirteen-year-old boy who had taken his own life due to excessive bullying. She remembered the caption from the boy's parents: "We never thought this could happen to our sweet Joshua. He was such a fun-loving kid who brought happiness everywhere he went."

She stopped stirring the soup and rushed upstairs to Logan's room. Through the door, she could hear him yelling, "STOP IT, STOP IT, STOP IT!"

She tried to open the door, but to her surprise, it was locked.

She began to panic. "LOGAN, YOU OPEN THIS DOOR RIGHT NOW! OPEN IT RIGHT NOW, DO YOU HEAR ME?!"

The few seconds it took for Logan to open the door felt like forever. When he finally opened the door, she barged in. Logan's face was beet red, he was sweating and shaking, and he must've just bitten his bottom lip as it was dripping with fresh blood.

She grabbed him and held him. Logan gave her a half-hearted hug in return. His phone continued dinging.

"Who's texting you?" she yelled.

Logan started to answer, but before he could, his phone dinged again as another message came in.

"Logan, give me that phone!" she demanded.

Logan, who rarely disrespected his mom, attempted to hide his phone, but with a quickness that surprised them both, she grabbed it before he could slip it into his pocket.

She typed in 1112, which was the passcode they agreed on when Logan was first given his phone, but it didn't work.

In a panic, she yelled, "TELL ME THE NEW PASSCODE!"

"3323," Logan said through his tears.

She angrily growled back, "Why in the world did you change it? What are you hiding from me?"

Before she could say another word, her eyes were drawn to the screen and her body tensed up so tight that she thought the phone might break right there in her hand as she read the words: "I HATE YOU, I HATE YOU!!!" "EVERYONE HATES YOU!" "WHY DON'T YOU DO US ALL A FAVOR AND DIE, JUST LIKE YOUR DAD DID!"

Her stomach dropped as if she'd been punched in the gut. She was afraid she might vomit.

The next text was a video of several kids shoving another kid down to the floor while other kids stood around watching. Some kids were taking pictures and videos with their phones, as others laughed and yelled out profanities.

At first, she couldn't see the kid on the floor who was trying to protect himself from two boys who were repeatedly kicking him as he lay there defenseless.

As the video continued, she recognized Doug and David, and when the camera circled back to the boy on the floor, her worst fears were realized. The boy on the floor, the boy who was being kicked in the stomach over and over, was her son, Logan.

Why was no one helping him? Why was everyone just standing around?

As the video ended, she could see Doug and David taking turns spitting in Logan's hair as he lay on the floor, crying in pain.

She dropped the phone, grabbed Logan, and began hugging him. She hugged him and hugged him, saying over and over again, "I love you, Logan. I Love You! You are a wonderful, amazing young man. You do not deserve this, and it is going to stop!"

The more she talked, the tighter she squeezed him. The tighter she squeezed him, the more she cried, and the more she cried, the tighter she squeezed him.

Molly couldn't imagine the pain her son was in. How alone he must've felt when he was begging for help and no one helped him. No one even tried to help.

"Logan, I am so sorry I wasn't there to help you! I'm so sorry!"

"It's okay, Mom, you didn't know."

"Why didn't you tell me?" she asked again.

"I didn't want you to worry."

She looked directly into Logan's eyes and said, "I am your mother; it's my job to worry!" She pulled him close and hugged him again and told him they would talk with the principal and the coach in the morning.

"No," Logan pleaded with his mom. "It would only make things worse."

She hugged Logan for several more minutes before grabbing her own phone.

"What are you doing, Mom?" Logan asked in a panic.

"I'm calling these boys' mothers."

"No, Mom, please don't. You'll only make things worse."

But, against Logan's wishes, she reluctantly called the mothers of the boys who had sent the text messages.

"Boys will be boys," one of the moms said.

Molly was beyond furious now, and against Logan's continued protests, she sent an email to Coach Jacobs, the school principal, and the superintendent, demanding a meeting with them. She wanted answers.

When they met with the principal, Molly showed him the video and the text messages and told him what was happening daily in the cafeteria, in the halls, and in the locker room. She wanted to know how this could happen to any kid in the school, not only her son. She wanted to know where the teachers and hall monitors were, and how often this happened to kids.

The principal appeared genuinely concerned.

He apologized for everything Logan and Molly had gone through and said he would take the appropriate actions to resolve the problem.

Molly and Logan left the meeting feeling hopeful but not at all convinced that the problem would be taken care of.

Later in the day, Molly received an email from Coach Jacobs, saying he would have a talk with the team about bullying and about sticking up for one another. She also received an email from the superintendent's office, saying they had discussed the situation with the school principal and would address the issue. The email emphasized the "no tolerance for bullying" policy but didn't say anything about protecting Logan or any other kid who was being bullied.

On the ride home, Molly asked Logan again why he didn't fight back or even try to defend himself. Logan said he was afraid of fighting back because the school policy said that any altercation, regardless of who started it, would result in a three-day suspension for both kids. He thought that if he didn't fight back, he wouldn't get in trouble, but he sure hoped that Doug and David would.

Doug and David got three days of in-school suspension and were suspended from the hockey team for those three days. If this was meant to deter Doug and David from future bullying, it sure didn't work. If anything, it only added to the problem because they couldn't care less about being suspended from school. Missing three days of hockey practice didn't bother them, either, because they already thought they were too good for practice.

Molly told Logan that she wouldn't care if he got suspended for trying to defend himself, but he should at least do something to try and stop it.

He told her about the one time in the locker room when he had finally had enough, so he shoved Doug and yelled "Stop it!"

But all that did was make things much worse, as Doug and David both jumped on him, knocked him to the floor, and then took turns rubbing his face on the locker room floor, telling him that he better never touch them again or things would get a lot worse, and they certainly had.

Molly slowly shook her head in frustration at herself. The clues had been there, like the various bruises on Logan's arms and the one time when he came home with the collar of his shirt torn and a bruise on his cheek. But when she asked him about it, he just said he was wrestling around and his shirt got accidentally torn and that he got hit in the face with a ball in PE class.

Molly knew she had to do something, and she remembered that her younger brother, Joe, had been bullied as a kid and took martial arts to learn how to defend himself. However, after a few years, their parents made him quit because he kept getting into fights.

Molly specifically remembered one fight and how scary it was. They were on the playground when a much bigger kid was picking on a group of smaller kids. Joe told the bigger kid to stop, and, without warning, the bigger kid kicked Joe in the groin. While Joe was on the ground, rolling around in pain, the bigger kid grabbed a smaller kid and threw him down on top of Joe. Then the bigger kid got in Joe's face, yelling, "Did that hurt, baby Joe?" Joe grabbed the bigger kid, tackled the kid to the ground, got on top of him, and repeatedly punched the kid in the face until an adult ran over and pulled him off.

The bigger kid got hurt pretty badly. Joe got in a lot of trouble and had to quit training in martial arts because of it.

Molly knew that had happened a long time ago. She also knew that Joe had spent time in Korea and had become an impressive martial artist. Now he traveled all over the world, teaching self-defense clinics. So she knew Joe could train Logan how to fight, but she was a little worried that Logan might only learn how to hurt someone. But after seeing the video and talking to the principal, it had become obvious that the coach and the school system weren't doing anything to protect Logan. At this point, she just wanted Logan to stop getting hurt, and Joe was her best hope.

Since Christmas break started the following week, Molly decided to let Logan stay home from school for the rest of the week and get an early start on his Christmas vacation. She thought the extra time away from school, and Doug and David, would be a good thing. Besides, her brother Joe was coming to town tomorrow, and she wanted Logan to get as much time with him as possible.

The next morning, she was in Logan's room early, waking him up. "Logan, get up, we've got a special day planned," she teased.

"Mom, you said I didn't have to go to school today," Logan said, pulling the covers over his head.

Molly started tickling Logan to wake him up. "I know, but we've got a special day planned."

"Mom, stop! What is it?" Logan was getting annoyed as he tried to keep his mom from tickling him.

"You'll see, but you need to get up, get a shower, and get ready."

As Logan stumbled out of bed, he wondered if they were selling the farm and moving, or maybe, someone was going to beat up Doug and David, and he could go back to playing the sport he loved without worrying about them ever again.

"What's the big surprise, Mom?"

"You'll see."

"Can you at least tell me where we're going?"

"That's a surprise too."

Soon they were pulling into the parking lot of Logan's favorite restaurant. "So, we're having breakfast? That's the big surprise?" Logan asked sarcastically.

"We're going to see someone who will change our lives and teach you how to defend yourself," she answered.

Logan looked puzzled, but before he could speak, he saw a man walking toward their car. He couldn't tell if he recognized him or not. The man wasn't that tall, but he appeared to be very muscular, and he was walking directly toward them. Logan squinted against the blinding sun. Then he cupped his hands over his eyes to block out the sun to get a better look at the approaching stranger.

As the man got closer, Logan got a little nervous; he couldn't take his eyes off him. Then, almost as if the man had blocked out the sun, Logan started to make out his face, was this ... no ... it couldn't be ... yes, it was, it was his Uncle Joe! Logan hurried out of the car just as his uncle approached.

Molly rushed around the front of the car, giving her brother a big hug. "Hey Joe, I've missed you. Thanks so much for coming."

"It's so good to see you. I'm glad to be here, sis," Joe replied.

As Logan stepped up to him, Joe extended his hand and said, "Logan, it's great to see you again, buddy."

Logan shook Joe's hand with a firm grip.

"That's an outstanding handshake you've got there, Logan, firm and strong!"

"Thank you," Logan said with a smile.

"You're welcome," Joe said, smiling back.

Molly and Joe spent a few minutes going over everything they had talked about on the phone. Molly said she didn't want Logan just learning how to fight; she wanted him to learn how to defend himself if he needed to but not just learn to beat someone up.

"Okay, Logan, this is the big, life-changing surprise I told you about. As you know, your Uncle Joe is a master martial artist and a self-defense expert. He's going to spend the next several weeks with us and teach you some tools to stop this bullying problem."

"Really, Mom?" Logan said as his eyes lit up.

"Really, Logan," Molly said as she leaned over and kissed him on the cheek. "Okay, boys, have fun. I'll see you later." Molly began to get into her car.

"Where are you going?" Logan asked.

"I've got some errands to run. I'll see you back home later."

"Okay," Logan said hesitantly.

"I love you," Molly said as she started her car.

"I love you too, Mom," Logan replied.

As Molly drove away, Joe asked, "So are you hungry?"

"For sure!" Logan replied.

"Good. Me too. Let's go eat."

They both smiled, walked into the restaurant, and took a seat in a corner booth. "Your mom tells me this is your favorite restaurant."

"Yes, it is," Logan replied.

"What's your favorite thing to eat here?"

"Pancakes!" Logan said with excitement.

"Awesome, I like pancakes too."

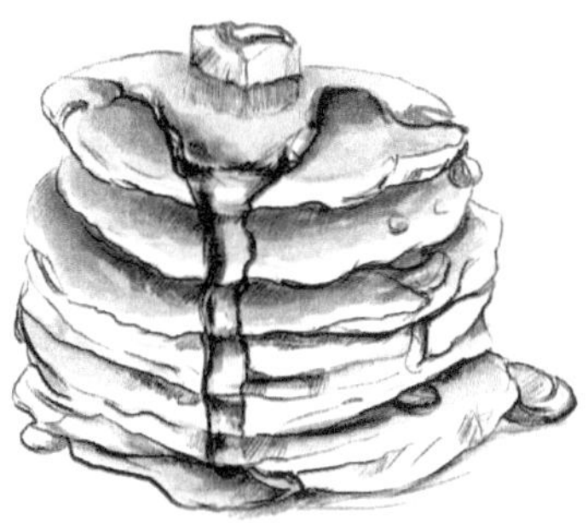

As they waited for their breakfast, Joe asked Logan about school, hockey, and how many girlfriends he had. Logan blushed about the girlfriend question. Then he got quiet and said that he was thinking about quitting hockey.

"Quitting hockey?" Joe asked. "I thought you loved hockey?"

"I do, it's just that ... I don't know, I don't think I like it anymore."

"Oh, I see. Did you know that your dad and I played hockey together?"

"Yeah, Mom told me. She said that Dad was really good, right?"

"Yes, he was really good. Your dad was the best player I ever played with."

Logan smiled. He loved hearing stories about his dad.

"Guess who else has the potential to be that good?"

"Who?" Logan asked.

"I'll give you a hint. He's sitting in this restaurant, he's wearing a black shirt, and he just ordered a large stack of pancakes."

A big smile came over Logan's face again. "Do you really think so?"

"I really do. Your mom told me how great of a player you are already. She is very proud of you. But one thing's for sure, you will never find out if you quit."

Logan's smile disappeared as he looked down. "I know, but ..."

"That's okay, Logan, that's why I'm here. I'm here to help you, buddy, and I promise you, things are going to be different for you."

Within a few minutes, their order arrived. Logan eagerly poured nearly half the bottle of syrup over his pancakes and dug in.

After their delicious breakfast, Joe paid the bill, and they headed out to his truck.

"Where are we going?" Logan asked.

"We're going to start your training," Joe replied.

"Right now?" Logan asked enthusiastically.

Joe nodded. "Absolutely, no time like the present."

"Are you going to teach me how to fight?" Logan asked.

"Why do you want to learn how to fight?"

"So I can be tough," Logan replied.

"Do you think fighting makes you tough?"

"Doesn't it?" Logan said tentatively as he hopped into the cab of Joe's truck.

"No, fighting doesn't make you tough," Joe said in a serious tone. "Fighting is something that fools and bullies do because they want to act tough. They think fighting will make them tough and gain them respect."

"You mean it doesn't?"

Joe shook his head side to side and asked, "What does respect mean to you?"

Logan shrugged his shoulders and said, "I don't know."

"Think about it. Who do you think of when you hear the word respect?"

"Um ... I think of ... a leader, I guess." Logan sounded unsure of his answer.

"Sure, what about a coach or a superhero?"

"Yeah, those too," Logan replied more confidently.

"Why do you think of them when you hear the word respect?" Joe asked.

"Because they are good people, and they help others," Logan replied.

"Do you respect these people because you want to be like them?"

"I guess so."

Joe nodded his head as he flipped on his blinker and got into the left turn lane before stopping at the traffic light. He looked over at Logan, who was adjusting the sun visor and the air vents and checking out Joe's cool stereo.

"Man, this is a nice truck," Logan said as he fiddled with the impressive stereo system.

Joe couldn't help but smile. "Logan, have you ever heard of Bruce Lee?"

"I think so. Wasn't he a karate guy?"

Joe chuckled, "Yes, he was a karate guy. He once said,

"Knowledge will give you power, but character gives you respect." Do you know what that means?

"I'm not sure," Logan said, obviously confused.

"Well, it's our first lesson, and it's a key to becoming bully proof," Joe proudly replied.

"Bully proof?" Logan asked.

"Becoming bully proof is as easy as ABC."

"What's as easy as ABC?" Logan asked.

"Becoming bully proof," Joe said, smiling.

"I'm confused," Logan said as he readjusted the sun visor.

"That's okay. I promise it's simple, but that doesn't mean it's going to be easy."

"Now I'm really confused," Logan said.

Joe smiled, then said, "First, I've got a couple of questions to ask. Are you willing to learn?"

Logan nodded his head yes.

"Are you willing to work hard and follow directions?"

"Sure," Logan proudly said.

"Good," Joe said with a smile. "I promise you this: if you promise to do your best, I'll take you on a journey over the next several weeks, and I'll share with you some of the best lessons I've learned over the past forty years in martial arts. How's that sound?"

Logan's eyes lit up. "That sounds great."

"But you must promise to always do your best and never give up, even when things get tough, especially when you feel like quitting. Do you think you can do that?" Joe asked.

"Is it going to be hard?" Logan asked in a concerned voice.

"Not any harder than getting bullied, but the reward is pretty awesome."

Logan didn't say anything; he just looked at Joe.

"So, what do you think, Logan? Are you ready to become bully proof?" Joe asked.

"I am," Logan confidently replied.

"Good," Joe said as he turned the truck right onto the rocky road that led to Logan's house.

CHAPTER 4

JOE STOPPED HIS TRUCK in front of the barn, and as they got out, they were immediately approached by several barn cats. Joe reached down and petted one that had wrapped itself around his leg.

"Is being bully proof like being a black belt?" Logan asked.

Joe smiled and laughed a bit as he shook his head side to side. "No, being bully proof and wearing a black belt are two totally different things. I'll tell you what my instructor told me many years ago. He said a belt is only good for holding up your pants."

Logan laughed and said, “No, I meant like a real black belt.”

“Sure, like the one I’m wearing.” Grinning, Joe pointed to the black belt he was wearing to hold up his pants.

“No, I mean like the people on TV, and like you, a karate black belt.”

Joe stood up from petting the cat and said, “Logan, this may come as a surprise to you, but not everyone who wears a ‘black belt’ is really a black belt, especially actors on TV.”

“Really?” Logan asked.

“Really,” Joe said. “I’ll tell you all about it while you show me around the farm. It’s been a while since I’ve been here. Sound good?”

Logan nodded his head yes. “Okay, well here’s the barn,” Logan said, laughing as he pointed at the barn.

“Looks like the barn door has seen better days,” Joe said, pointing out some missing boards.

“It’s been that way for a while. I tried to fix it myself, but I think we need some new boards.”

Joe nodded in agreement. “Let’s plan a day to work on the door. But first, keep showing me around the farm, and I’ll tell you more about my martial arts training and, most importantly, how to gain respect.”

“That sounds good,” Logan said excitedly.

As they pulled the big barn door open, Joe was taken back to when he was a kid. He remembered helping his dad build the barn and the big barn doors. Everything looked much smaller now. It’s amazing how much smaller things appear when you're looking through the eyes of an adult instead of a child, he realized.

Joe got caught up in his thoughts, thinking about all the times he shoveled the horse poop out of the stalls and got hay down from the top of the barn. Time seemed to stand still as he reflected.

"Right this way, Uncle Joe," Logan said as he pointed to the loft where the hay bales were kept.

"Wow, I was just thinking back to when I was a kid and how many times I had to shovel those stalls. It seems so long ago. It also looks like they could use a good shoveling now," Joe said as he playfully shook his head.

"Yeah, I was going to get to that," Logan said, feeling a little embarrassed at how messy the stalls were.

As they continued walking through the barn, Logan asked, "So, how many fights have you been in, Uncle Joe?"

Joe looked at Logan. "Fighting is never a good thing, especially if it can be avoided. As a matter of fact, fighting is one of the reasons I had to quit martial arts the first time."

"Why did you have to quit?" Logan asked.

"Well, I got into a fight and hurt a kid pretty bad, plus I was playing hockey at the same time and started fighting a lot on the ice, so my parents thought that I was only learning how to hurt people. But the truth is martial arts had nothing to do with it. I had some built-up anger and rage from being bullied, and when this bigger kid attacked me and a smaller kid, I completely lost control of myself."

"What happened?"

"We were at the park, and this kid kept picking on me and some of the younger kids who were much smaller than he was. He would push them down and push them off the swings and then laugh when they started crying. I told him to stop it and quit picking on little kids. I guess this made him mad because without warning, he ran up and kicked me straight in the groin."

"Ow!!!" Logan said, making the face that all guys make at the thought of being kicked "there." "What did you do?" Logan asked.

"Well, the first thing I did was fall to my knees in pain. But, when he grabbed a smaller kid and threw him down on top of me, I lost it. I tackled the big kid to the ground and started hitting him, and I didn't stop until an adult came running over and pulled me off him."

Logan looked up at Joe in surprise.

"I ended up hurting the kid pretty bad, and my parents, your grandma and grandpa, pulled me out of martial arts because they thought I was only learning how to hurt people, and at the time, maybe they were right. Anyway, it didn't bother me too much because I was still focused on becoming a pro hockey player."

"You wanted to be a pro hockey player too?" Logan asked. Uncle Joe was full of surprises, he thought.

"I did, and I worked extremely hard at it, but when I turned nineteen, I had to accept the hard reality that it just wasn't going to happen. I wasn't going to become a pro hockey player."

"Why not?" Logan asked.

"I just wasn't good enough. I discovered there is a huge difference between being a really good amateur player and becoming a professional athlete."

"Oh," Logan said as the smile left his face.

"It's okay, Logan, this was one of many lessons I've learned in life. We don't always know the answers to why things work out the way they do. But I do know this: if I would've become a professional hockey player, I probably wouldn't be here right now with you, helping you become bully proof."

Logan nodded his head. He was really happy that Joe was here. "Is that when you started back in martial arts?"

Joe smiled. "It is. I picked myself back up from that crushing defeat and turned all my attention toward training in martial arts."

Joe paused and continued, "I became obsessed with it. I went to class every time the doors were open. All I could think about was becoming a black belt, and after many years of intense daily training, I finally tested for my black belt."

"Did you pass, is that when you got your black belt?" Logan asked excitedly.

"No, I actually failed my first black belt test."

"No way!" Logan was shocked.

"I did."

"Wow, I never knew that. What happened?"

"Well, I was young and immature, and I thought I knew everything about being a black belt. I thought being a black belt was about being strong, tough, physically fit, and knowing how to fight and kick butt."

"Well, isn't it?" Logan asked.

"Sure, that's part of it, but it's much more than that. I just didn't know that back then. What I did know was that, deep down in my heart, I was still that scared, intimidated little kid who had gained some self-confidence from years of tough physical training but not much of anything else. I soon found out the hard way how fragile my self-confidence and self-esteem were."

"What happened?" Logan asked, eager to hear more.

"Well, as a young guy in my early twenties, I had few real-life experiences. All I really knew was that I was bullied as a kid for most of my teen years, and I was still hurting a bit from having my hockey dreams crushed. I guess I kinda felt like life was bullying me, just like everyone else was. I just knew that things were about to change because I was about to become a black belt. In my mind, that was a license to beat up anyone who tried to pick on me or bully me again."

Joe paused and looked directly at Logan. "I remember training so hard and telling myself that I wouldn't fail at this so that I wouldn't be bullied ever again. I would picture the bully's face every time I threw a technique, then I would throw it harder and harder, each time digging deeper to get more power on each movement. I would push myself to the physical limit, knowing that one day I would have my chance to set things straight with the guys who had hurt me. I truly believed that when I got my black belt, everything would be different."

Logan looked at Joe, hanging on every word he said.

Joe continued, "Logan, I learned a very valuable lesson that day and many days since then, and that's why I want you to become more than just a tough guy who can kick butt. I want you to have something I never had at your age; I want you to have true, long-lasting self-confidence and self-respect. I want you to truly believe in yourself, to confidently stand up for what is right, and to courageously protect yourself and anyone else who's in need. What I'm going to teach you is far more important than earning a belt or just learning how to fight."

"Okay ... wow!" Logan said, his mind racing with thoughts. "But what about beating up the guys who are mean to me?" Logan looked down to the ground and then back up at Joe.

"Beating someone up who is mean to you is not being bully proof, it's just beating someone up. If you go around beating up everyone who makes you mad, your life will turn into one big continuous fight, and that's the furthest thing from being bully proof."

Logan looked back to the ground and shuffled his feet. "I know, but ..."

Joe interrupted, "I know this is hard to understand after what you've been through. To be truthful, I don't know if I would've fully understood this at your age, either, but I'm going to do my best to plant these thoughts, these seeds in your mind, to help you understand and, most importantly, help you grow to become your very best."

Logan nodded his head, even though he didn't totally understand what Joe was saying. He could tell that Uncle Joe cared, and he was grateful that he was here to help, so Logan agreed and told himself that he would do his very best.

As they walked out of the barn and headed toward the field, they stopped and took in the beautiful sight. The sun was directly overhead, and they could see the beauty of the pasture with their horses and cows grazing in it.

"Logan, do you know what self-respect is?"

"Um ... it's when you respect yourself," Logan said with an unsure grin.

"Sure, that's part of it. I like to think that self-respect is the starting point for all great achievements in your life. If you think about it, it's really pretty simple. If you don't respect yourself, then you will never be able to respect anyone else."

Logan paused and then said, "Do you think that's why some kids bully me, because they don't respect themselves?"

"Logan, that is spot on. You see, self-respect is based on a person's self-worth, basically, how a person feels about themselves. If they feel good about themselves, then they will likely treat others with respect and kindness. However, if they don't feel good about themselves, then they will likely disrespect others and treat them poorly, even bully them."

As they walked farther out into the pasture where the horses were grazing, they were approached by a colt, who nudged Logan on the shoulder.

"This is my favorite horse ... his name is Smokey," Logan said as he rubbed Smokey's head and petted him on the side of the neck. Smokey tilted his head to the side, showing his appreciation.

Logan told Joe about how he remembered the day Smokey was born and how he watched him grow up and about all the hard work he put in to tame Smokey enough to ride him.

Before long, two other horses came over, looking for attention and possibly a sugar cube. They sniffed around for a bit and, realizing there were no treats, slowly walked away. The cows kept doing their own thing. Some were eating grass, and others were just standing around basking in the sun.

"So, was it hard work taming Smokey?" Joe asked.

"Yes, it was a lot of work."

"I know it was, and I've always believed that the best way to establish your self-worth is through good old-fashioned hard work to earn something or achieve a goal."

Logan nodded his head, saying, "Oh, like me working hard to tame Smokey so I could ride him."

"Exactly, Logan! I know it wasn't easy, and I'm sure there were many times that you got frustrated and wanted to give up, but you had a goal of being able to ride Smokey, so you worked hard toward that goal and didn't quit."

"It was a lot of work, and Smokey was stubborn, but my dad told me that the hard work would all be worth it when I was able to ride Smokey without him trying to buck me off."

Joe put up his hand for a high five and said, "Logan, you're amazing. That's exactly the point I'm making. You have to put in the hard work to get the reward you're looking for. But the real reward is the self-respect you gain during the process."

As Joe continued, Logan remembered how great he felt the day he actually rode Smokey without the colt trying to throw him off.

"You know, Logan, one of the saddest things that happens to kids, and even adults, is when they get something for nothing. When they get rewarded for something they didn't earn."

"Like getting a trophy for coming in last place?" Logan asked as he looked up at Joe.

"That's exactly what I'm talking about. Sure, they may get a temporary good feeling from getting something for free, but in the end, it doesn't help build their self-worth or self-respect. As a matter of fact, it does the complete opposite and actually causes people to bully themselves."

"Bully themselves?" Logan asked.

"Yes, bully themselves. If you get into a habit of expecting something for nothing, then you end up developing a very difficult habit to break. And, living with bad habits is essentially bullying yourself."

"Wow, I never thought of it that way," Logan replied.

Joe smiled, "Maybe not, but your dad did. That's why he taught you to never give up on training Smokey. That's also why he taught you to work hard around the farm. He was teaching you lessons about self-respect without you even knowing it."

"I do work hard around the farm, and I work hard to get good grades, and I really work hard at being a good hockey player," Logan confidently replied. He tilted his head to the side and glanced up at Joe. "I know that most of the kids on the hockey team don't have any chores, and I have to do all this work around here."

Joe nodded his head, showing that he understood. "I know it doesn't seem fair now, but I promise you, it will make all the difference in the world when you get older."

Logan didn't say anything, but Joe saw the disbelief on Logan's face, so he continued. "You see, too often, kids and adults get things in life that they didn't work for; like you said, they get a trophy for coming in last place, or they get to play their favorite position just because their dad is the coach."

"I know what you mean. I had a couple of boys on my baseball team who threw fits and were terrible sports, but they still got to play shortstop and bat first because their dads were the coaches."

"Unfortunately, this goes on every single day, and as unfair as it appears to everyone else, it is even more unfair to the person who is given something they didn't earn.

They are the ones who grow up thinking they're entitled to anything they want, without putting in the work. They will expect to get a job, or a car, or a nice house, just because. But that's just not how life works. There's an old saying: there's no such thing as a free lunch. This means there is a cost for everything, nothing in life is free, and sooner or later, you'll have to pay the price. And, that's why you have these chores, so you can learn these lessons now, at an early age, because the older you get, the harder these lessons are to learn."

They stopped walking when they could see the barbwire fence that marked the end of their property.

"I guess I understand, but it sure doesn't seem fair now," Logan said as he looked at Joe.

"It will soon, and you'll know it when it happens," Joe said confidently. "So, you want to race to the end of the field?" Joe asked as he started running.

"No fair!" Logan cried out at Joe's head start.

"Come on, Logan, you can catch me!" Joe yelled, looking back but not slowing his pace.

They ran to the end of the field and stopped right in front of the barbwire fence. "You're pretty fast, Logan. You could've beaten me if I hadn't had that lead on you."

"Thanks. I'm one of the fastest skaters on my hockey team," Logan said breathlessly.

"I don't doubt that. You've got some strong legs from walking these fields and doing all your chores on the farm. I bet you're one of the strongest kids on your team too."

Logan kicked at the dirt and said, "I can do more push-ups than anyone on the team."

Joe raised his hand up high over his head for another high five, and Logan jumped up and hit Joe's hand with a "SMACK."

"Okay, Logan, quick review, our first lesson was what?" Joe asked.

"Respect!" Logan said confidently.

"And why is respect so important?" Joe asked.

"Because if I don't respect myself, then it's hard for anyone else to respect me," Logan replied.

"Wow! That's exactly right. I work with some adults who don't get it that quickly. Nice work."

Logan's smile showed how proud he was of himself.

"Are you ready to race back to the barn?" Joe asked as he pretended to take off.

"All the way to the barn?" Logan asked.

"Sure, or at least until one of us runs out of breath."

"Okay then, you're on," Logan said as he took off.

"Hey!" Joe yelled out.

Logan had the lead, but Joe quickly caught up with him, and they were neck and neck. Joe wasn't cutting Logan any slack as he encouraged him to run faster.

"I'm going to beat you, Logan. You better hurry up," Joe said as they got closer and closer to the barn. By then, Logan had started to slow down. "Don't stop now. There's only a little bit more to go," Joe continued.

"I'm almost out of breath," Logan said, gasping.

"Yeah, me too, but I'm not going to quit and neither are you." But, just as the words were coming out of Joe's mouth, Logan slowed down and then stopped completely. Joe turned around and jogged back to Logan.

Logan was breathing heavy. He stood there with his head down and his shoulders slouched forward, looking totally defeated.

"What's up, Logan? You almost had me."

"I just ran out of breath," Logan said without looking up but clearly disappointed in himself.

"I get it, I know it's tough, and I know you're tired and breathing heavy, but we've only got a little more to go, and we're going to finish strong," Joe said encouragingly.

"Okay, but do we have to run?" Logan asked, still breathing heavy.

"We are going to finish strong because I want you to form a habit of never quitting on yourself. A solid way to build self-respect is by always finishing what you start. So, we are going to at least jog the rest of the way. Okay?"

"Okay," Logan said while still catching his breath.

They jogged the rest of the way to the barn, with Joe encouraging Logan to keep going and not give up. As they made their way back to the barn, they saw Molly standing on the front porch and waving them over. The unseasonably warm December weather was perfect for the type of outdoor training Joe had planned for Logan.

"What have you boys been up to?" Molly asked as she handed them each a glass of water and a turkey sandwich and sat down on the porch swing. "Have you learned anything yet?"

"Well, Mom, I learned that I need to always finish what I start, work hard, and not give up on myself."

Joe nodded his head, acknowledging Logan's answer. "Nice job, Logan, and why is that important?" he asked.

"Um ..." Logan mumbled, trying to remember the answer.

"What do you gain from working hard and not giving up? "Self ..." Joe said, leading him to the answer.

"Self-respect!" Logan yelled out.

"That's right, Logan, self-respect, and self-respect is the first step to becoming bully proof."

Molly looked over at Logan and smiled.

"Are you ready for the next lesson?" Joe asked.

"Sure," Logan said after guzzling a long drink of water.

"This lesson is the most basic law of the universe. Any idea what it is?" Joe asked.

Logan shook his head side to side with a confused expression and looked over at Molly. "Do you know, Mom?"

Molly smiled and said, "Is it sowing and reaping?" not sounding too confident in her answer.

"Winner, we have a winner!" Joe kidded his sister. "Yes, it's the law of sowing and reaping. Which means, what you put in is what you'll get out. And, if you put nothing in, then you really can't expect to get anything out."

When they finished their sandwiches, Joe began explaining the law of sowing and reaping and how it applies to the thoughts in our minds. "Think about a farmer. If he doesn't put seeds in the ground in the spring, can he expect a harvest in the fall?"

"I guess not," Logan said, sounding a bit confused.

"Of course not. If you put nothing in, can you really expect to get something out?"

"No, I guess you can't," Logan was now sounding a little more confident, but he was still not sure of Joe's point.

"Just look at the farmer's field across the road. I'm sure a few months ago, that field was full. What did they grow this year?"

"Corn," Logan answered. "I always think it's cool when the corn starts to grow, and then suddenly it's taller than I am, and then it's gone."

The three of them sat on the front porch, looking at the farmer's bare field. It was a bright sunny day with a nice cool breeze, and the view from the front porch was very peaceful.

Joe continued, "So, for the farmer to have his corn in the fall, what does he need to do in the spring?"

"He has to plant the seeds," Logan replied.

"Boom! That's right," Joe said.

Logan and Molly looked at each other and smiled.

"Basically, respect works the same way. If you don't put anything into respecting yourself, you will never be able to show respect to anyone else because nothing in, equals ...?" Joe paused for Logan to finish the sentence.

"Nothing out," Logan replied.

Joe smiled and pumped his fist in agreement. "Yes! And your mind's garden works the same way."

"My mind's garden?" Logan asked.

"Yes, your mind's garden."

Logan leaned back on his elbows and draped his legs off the edge of the porch, all the time watching his uncle with curiosity.

Joe continued, "Would you agree that if you put an onion seed in the ground, then an onion plant is what you're going to get?"

"Sure," Logan answered.

"Would you agree that if you put a strawberry seed in the ground, then you're going to get a strawberry plant?"

"Of course."

"Would you also agree that there is no way to get a juicy strawberry if you've planted an onion seed?"

"Yes, I agree." Logan was laughing, but he was still wondering where Uncle Joe was going with all this.

"So, just to make sure we're clear, if I want strawberries, what kind of seeds do I have to plant?" Joe asked.

"Strawberry seeds," Logan confidently replied.

"Correct, and if I want onions, what kind of seeds do I have to plant?"

"Onion seeds."

"Pretty simple, right?"

"Sure," Logan said, looking over at his mom to see if she understood what Joe was saying. Molly didn't say anything; she just smiled and winked at Logan.

"Your mind's garden is the most fertile garden in the world, and it grows whatever you put in it. Your thoughts are the seeds in your mind's garden, and whatever thoughts you plant, either good or bad, happy or sad, positive or negative, are the seeds that will grow in your mind. So, if you plant negative thoughts all day long, what do you think you're going to get?"

"More negative thoughts," Logan replied.

"Right, and the same is true if you believe any of the negative, mean, and hateful things that a few mean kids might say about you. This is why you must be extremely careful about what thoughts you allow into your mind. Once those seeds are planted, they begin to grow, and the more they grow, the bigger they get. Before long, you will start to believe those negative thoughts about yourself."

"So, I have to be careful what thoughts I allow into my mind," Logan said as he shook his head, acknowledging that he understood.

"That's exactly right! Because what you plant is ..." Joe paused again, allowing Logan to finish the sentence.

"What you get," Logan finished.

"Boom!" Joe said, punching the air with his right hand.

A huge smile spread across Logan's face as he looked over to his mom for confirmation.

Joe got up from the porch and stretched down to touch his toes.

Molly also stood up, grabbed the empty water glasses, and asked, "So, what's next, boys?"

Joe twisted side to side to stretch his back and answered, "Oh, I thought about continuing our lesson on the law of sowing and reaping. Do you still have a garden out back?"

"Well, we did, but now it's just full of weeds," Molly replied.

"So you've got a weed garden?" Joe said with a big grin on his face.

"I guess you could say that," Molly replied as they walked down the steps toward the back of the house.

"Unfortunately, that's the exact same thing that can happen with our mind's garden if we don't pay attention. It can get taken over by the weeds," Joe said, looking over at Logan and Molly.

"Weeds in my mind?" Logan asked.

"Absolutely, the worst kind of weeds too: fear, negativity, self-doubt, anger, and jealousy."

While walking to the back of the house, Joe pointed out a weed growing in the middle of the rock driveway. "Did you plant that weed there?" he asked, looking at Logan.

"No, of course not," Logan replied.

"Then how did it get there?"

"I don't know," Logan said, shrugging his shoulders. "I guess it just grew there."

"Well, that's a lesson in itself; weeds will pop up and grow anywhere, just like those negative, ugly thoughts that can pop up anytime in your mind."

Logan began to wonder how many weeds he had in his mind's garden. "Is there a way to stop these weeds from growing in my mind's garden?" Logan asked.

"Undoubtedly, and that's exactly what we're going to work on, but first I want you to experience firsthand how hard it is digging up weeds in a real garden."

"Wait, what?" Logan asked. He looked at Uncle Joe to see if he was serious.

"Wow, that is quite a weed garden you're growing. We're going to need a gardening hoe, a rake, and a shovel," Joe said, looking over at Logan. "And a couple pairs of gloves."

Logan was back in a few minutes with the tools Joe asked for.

"Do you know how to dig up weeds?" Joe asked, pointing to the gardening hoe.

"I guess so," Logan replied.

"Show me how it's done." Joe grinned as he pointed to the patch of weeds.

Logan laid down the rake and the shovel and took the gardening hoe and began digging at the weeds. He dug and dug and dug, and within a couple of minutes, he was sweating like crazy. "How many weeds do I have to dig up?"

"Well, you've got about five dug up so far, so it looks like we have got about a hundred and fifty to go," Joe said with a smile.

Logan looked up and gave Joe a halfhearted smile as he wiped the sweat from his forehead. "This is hard work."

"May I show you an easier way?" Joe asked.

"Yes, please!" Logan said, giving the hoe to Joe.

"Try it like this." Joe dug the hoe deep into the ground to get under the bottom of the weed, and then with one motion, pulled up the entire weed all at once. "Do you see how I did that, Logan? This will save you a lot of time and effort and is another lesson in itself. It's learning to work smarter, not harder."

"That's something my dad would always tell me," Logan said as he took the tool back from Joe.

"Okay, great," Joe said, pointing to another area of the garden. "Try it over here then, on this patch of weeds. Another valuable lesson to remember is, 'teamwork makes the dream work.' So let's work together on this thing and accomplish twice as much." He picked up the rake and told Logan to dig up the weeds with the gardening hoe while he used the rake to rake the weeds out of the soil.

A few hours later, the sun was starting to set. Logan couldn't believe how fast the day had gone by. He had learned a lot in a short amount of time and was thinking about what Joe had said, that hard work helps you develop self-respect because you are focused on doing your best, and that effort helps you feel better about yourself. No doubt about it, after the hard work today, he was feeling better about himself.

They dug up weeds for a while longer, then cleaned off the tools and put them back in the barn. In the barn, Logan showed Joe how he did his evening chores before heading into the house for dinner.

When Logan sat down at the table, it was obvious that something was bothering him.

"What's wrong, Logan?" Molly asked.

"I don't know, Mom. I mean I felt great all day spending time and working with Uncle Joe, but now my mind is going back to Doug and David. I keep thinking about all the mean things they've done and said to me, and I guess I'm just scared that I'll never be able to stop them."

Molly looked over at Joe and said, "That's why your Uncle Joe is here."

Joe smiled at Molly and nodded his head in appreciation. "I get it, buddy. Did you know that Doug and David's dads used to bully me when I was younger?"

"What ... their dads bullied you?" Logan asked in disbelief.

"They did. They bullied me as a kid and as a teenager, and they would probably still try to bully me today if I saw them."

"Wait ... adults bully people too?" Logan asked.

"Sure, what do you think happens to bullies when they grow up?" Joe replied.

"I don't know, I just thought maybe they grew up and realized it was wrong."

"You're awesome, Logan. But unfortunately, most of the time, they grow up and keep doing the same things to bully others. Then they have kids who follow in their footsteps, and the cycle continues."

"Wow, I sure wouldn't have thought that anyone ever bullied you," Logan said. He was looking at Joe's muscular arms.

Joe smiled again. "I'm a human being and, unfortunately, every human being has been bullied or will probably be bullied at one time or another in their life. The difference between now and then is that I've mastered the ABCs to become bully proof. And so will you."

"What are the ABCs?" Logan said as he perked up.

"That's what I'm going to teach you. But before we can learn the ABCs, we have to make sure that our mind's garden is ready to receive the knowledge. Just like we had to dig up all the weeds in your real garden before we could plant the seeds, we also have to do the same thing with our mind's garden."

"So how do we do that?" Logan asked.

"Well, we've already been working on it with the first couple lessons from today. Do you remember what they are?"

"Um ... I remember the garden example, and before that, we talked about hard work and self-respect, and before that, we ... talked about not giving up on myself."

"Very good, Logan. I'm very proud of you. That's a great memory you have," Joe replied, obviously impressed.

Molly, who had been sitting next to Logan, gave him a big squeeze and kissed him on the cheek. "That's awesome, Logan."

Logan smiled. "Thanks, Mom."

During dinner, Joe repeated how important it is to protect your mind's garden from the negative weeds of society and the negative thoughts that bullies try to plant in your mind. He described how bullies try to plant fear, intimidation, self-doubt, and any other negative thoughts to control you. Even though we can't control the thoughts, words, and actions of others, we can control how we respond to them. We choose to believe them or not. He said everyone struggles with their own challenges at different stages of their life, but regardless of what stage of life you're in, you still have the ability to control the seeds and weeds that you grow in your mind's garden.

Logan and Molly listened attentively to everything Joe was saying. Logan got it; he visualized his brain with big weeds sticking out and him plucking the weeds one by one. Logan looked down and then asked, "Uncle Joe, why do you think Doug and David bully me?"

"Logan, there are probably a hundred reasons why kids bully other kids. The most common reason is that it's learned behavior. Another reason is pure jealousy. Or maybe they are so unhappy with themselves that they think hurting someone else and taking away that person's happiness will somehow make them feel better about themselves."

Logan tilted his head to the side. "I don't think other kids, especially Doug and David, are jealous of me."

"I would bet they are. Because they see someone as awesome as you are, who is sharp, handsome, has strong muscles, and a great personality, plus you've got an incredible mom, and you're an amazing hockey player. Of course, they're jealous."

"I guess," Logan said, but he clearly didn't think so.

"I want you to remember this: you can't control what other kids think, or do, or say about you. The only thing and only person you have control over is you. So be sure to always do the right thing and plant the right seeds in your mind's garden, and I promise you'll start to believe in yourself. Then it won't matter what other kids think or say about you because you will know the truth about yourself, and that's all that matters."

"You really think so?"

"I know so, but it will take a little time. Just like planting a seed today, it will take some time for that seed to grow. I promise you this: we are going to plant the seeds of self-worth, self-confidence, and self-respect, and we are going to water those seeds daily for the next few weeks with lessons, drills, and workouts until you not only believe in yourself, but most importantly, you become bully proof."

When Joe finished speaking, Logan looked at his mom and then over at Joe and said, "I'm ready."

Joe reached over and gave them each a high five.

After finishing dinner, Logan asked, "Uncle Joe, did you say that Doug and David's dads bullied you?"

"Yes, they bullied me a lot when I was younger."

"What did you do about it? I bet you beat them up," Logan said, followed by "Pow" as he threw an imaginary punch through the air.

"No. I actually did the worst thing I could do. I didn't do anything."

"You didn't do anything either? Why not?" Logan asked, thinking this sounded a lot like his life.

"Mostly because I was scared," Joe replied.

"You were afraid of them? I can't imagine you being afraid of anyone."

"I was, and what made things worse was that I allowed them to plant those negative weeds in my mind, and instead of digging them up, I just let them grow. Before long, those negative weeds controlled my mind and the way I felt about myself."

Joe paused then continued, "I allowed those weeds to grow into something so scary that I was afraid to do anything. I became frozen with fear. Those weeds of fear, intimidation, and self-doubt had become so strong and so powerful that they killed all of my confidence and self-respect. Just like the weeds in your real garden, they suffocated all the good seeds and took over."

Logan's eyes lit up. "That's exactly what's happening to me right now. They've got me so scared that I don't know what to do. That's why I want to quit the hockey team because I'm so afraid of them."

"Well, I promise you, buddy, this is where it ends. This cycle of bullying ends now!"

Logan and Molly could see the look in Joe's eyes and hear the determination in his voice, and for the first time in a long time, they truly felt like there was hope.

Logan fell asleep feeling really good that his Uncle Joe was here and excited to see what tomorrow would bring. Down the hall, in his old childhood room, Joe felt a deep calm come over his mind and body. It was like a second chance to redo the past. He could be the hero he never had, while guiding Logan on how to become a hero of his own life.

Joe smiled to himself, and just before he fell asleep, his last thought was: *This cycle of bullying ends now.*

CHAPTER 5

THE NEXT MORNING, Joe took advantage of the beautiful sunrise to go for a jog around the farm. By the time Logan made it downstairs, Joe was finishing up breakfast.

"Good morning, Logan. How ya feeling?" Joe asked.

Molly chimed in, "Good morning, hon."

"Good morning, Uncle Joe, good morning, Mom. I'm feeling good," Logan said with a smile.

Molly walked over to give Logan a hug and a kiss on the cheek and handed him a plate of bacon and eggs.

Joe finished his last drink of orange juice and turned to Logan. "How about I show you a few techniques, and then you walk me through your morning chores after breakfast?"

"Sure, Uncle Joe. That would be great," Logan said as he took a bite of his eggs.

After breakfast, they headed outside and Joe spent the next thirty minutes walking Logan through a series of punches, kicks, and defensive motions in the front yard. Logan repeated the series of movements several times each.

"Nice work, Logan. That's really good. You pick up things quickly."

Logan smiled and continued practicing the front kicks he had just learned.

"That's a great start. We'll get back to this later, but right now, we've got some chores to do," Joe said with a smile.

"Okay," Logan agreed.

"So, what's first?" Joe asked.

Logan led Joe to the barn while telling him about his morning chores, including filling up the water trough and feeding the horses and cows. He told Joe he gave them grain in the morning and hay at night so that he didn't get hay all over his clothes before school.

As they finished up the chores, Joe said, "I'm very happy to see you up early and doing your chores. I'm also very impressed with how thorough you are. This is the type of respect I was talking about yesterday. You are showing respect for yourself by doing a great job. You're also respecting your mom by doing your chores without being asked."

Logan nodded his head and smiled, showing his appreciation. "Thank you, Uncle Joe. I know it makes my mom happy."

As they walked out of the barn, Logan turned to Joe and asked, "I know you're teaching me to become bully proof, but will I also learn how to fight?"

"Why do you want to learn how to fight?" Joe responded.

"So I can be tough," Logan replied.

Joe stopped walking and looked at Logan. "You're already tough. I guarantee you're tougher than any of those kids at school, and I promise you're much tougher than Doug and David."

"I am?" Logan asked. Uncle Joe had confused him again.

"Absolutely you are! You just need the confidence to believe it."

Logan wondered if his Uncle Joe really thought that or if he just said it to make him feel better.

Logan's thoughts were interrupted by Joe asking, "What makes you think that you're not tough?"

"Because I'm afraid," Logan said softly.

"I was afraid, too, when I was your age, and instead of telling anyone, I just kept it all to myself. I packed all the pain and suffering inside and tried to act like it didn't bother me, but the truth is, it did bother me. It bothered me so much that I began to hate myself, and I began to think that somehow I deserved this," Joe said with a serious tone. "The more I thought I deserved it, the more I hated myself, and the more I hated myself, the worse things got. It became an endless cycle of self-bullying and being bullied by others."

Logan stood there with his mouth open in shock, thinking to himself, "How could this strong, muscular martial arts expert ever be bullied by anyone? If someone like Uncle Joe was bullied, then how in the world is there any hope for me?"

Joe continued, "I lived with this fear for the majority of my life, and the longer I lived with it, the harder it was for me to break free from it."

"Just like digging up those weeds in the garden. I get it," Logan said while nodding his head.

"That's exactly right, Logan. Great job making the connection."

Logan smiled. He was proud of himself for figuring it out.

"You see, Logan, those weeds of negativity, fear, intimidation, and self-doubt had firmly taken root in my mind's garden, and it took me years to finally gain any self-respect and even longer to start believing in myself. That is the main reason why I do what I do and why I'm here with you. I want you and others to learn from my past experiences and have the tools that I never had."

Logan couldn't imagine that anyone else had gone through what he was going through. Yet, here was Uncle Joe, describing the same pain that he had felt for many years and the battles he was fighting now.

"So what do you boys have planned for the day?" Molly asked from the porch swing.

"I noticed some trails out behind the farm, and I thought I'd ask Logan if he wants to go for a hike and learn about the two wolves," Joe replied.

"The two wolves?" Logan asked.

"That sounds like a great idea," Molly said, winking at Logan.

They packed a backpack and headed out to the trail. The sun was shining brightly, and with a nip of coolness in the air, it was the perfect day for a hike in the woods.

"Are you ready for the next lesson?" Joe asked.

"Is it the two wolves?" Logan asked curiously.

"It is. But before we get to that, I've got a question for you."

"Okay," Logan replied.

"Do you know who's the biggest, meanest bully you'll ever face?"

Logan paused. "Um ... is it Doug?"

Joe shook his head no.

"Is it David?"

Joe again shook his head no, then replied, "It's the person who knows you better than anyone else. And it's the same person who you see in the mirror every single day."

"Me?!" Logan asked in surprise.

"Yes, it's you. And when I look in the mirror, it's me, and when your mom looks in the mirror, it's her, and when Doug and David look in the mirror, it's them."

Logan stopped walking and looked at Joe. "I don't understand. How can I be the biggest, meanest bully?"

"I'm about to tell you, and the answer is in the story of the two wolves."

Logan scratched his head, looking baffled, as they continued walking.

"You see, Logan, most people live their life being afraid. They live in fear of almost everything. They fear change, they fear anything new, and they fear what could possibly go wrong. They fear what they don't know."

"That's a lot of fear," Logan blurted out.

"It is, and did you know that we are only born with two real fears and that we learn all the other fears?"

"Really? ... Just two?" Logan asked.

"Yes, just two. Do you want to guess what they are?"

"Um ... snakes and bullies?" Logan said with a grin.

"Good guesses, and truthfully, I've been plenty afraid of both of those things." Joe paused, waiting for Logan to make another guess.

After a few seconds, Logan responded, "Um ... I'm not sure."

Joe smiled and said, "The only two natural fears we are born with are the fear of falling and the fear of loud noises."

"Really? I would've never guessed those," Logan replied.

"Neither would I, but it's true. All the other fears, as

scary as they may be, have been taught to us from other people or from our own experiences, or are simply made up in our minds."

Logan nodded his head, acknowledging Joe's point as they continued to walk down the trail.

"Some fears are really helpful to keep us safe, like when your mom taught you not to play in the street, or when you touched the hot stove as a toddler and got burned. But other fears aren't so helpful," Joe went on, "like being afraid that kids at school won't like you if you don't do what they do or being afraid to stand up to a bully."

"I've been afraid of both of those things," Logan replied.

"So have I, but here's something I've learned: if you don't learn to stand up to these fears now, then you'll be battling them your entire life. And that's why the first wolf's name is 'Fear.'"

Logan stopped walking and picked up a stick. "So the first wolf is named Fear."

Joe nodded. "Want to guess what the second wolf's name is?"

Logan poked his stick in the ground, and then looked up at Uncle Joe. "I'm not sure."

"The second wolf's name is Faith," Joe said as they came to a bend in the trail. "Have you ever seen any wolves out here?"

"No, I never have, but I haven't really explored these woods. My dad told me to always stay on the trail up here and not wander off in the woods."

Joe nodded and said, "Well, let's stick to the trail, and maybe we can find a nice spot to have lunch and finish learning about the two wolves."

"That sounds good to me, I'm getting hungry," Logan replied as he rubbed his stomach.

The two of them walked on for another fifteen minutes until they found a big opening in the trail. A small field separated the trail, and it was the perfect place to stop for lunch.

"How's this spot?" Joe asked.

"Looks good to me," Logan said as he pulled off the backpack. Logan had voluntarily carried the backpack, even though it was a little heavy. He wanted to show his Uncle Joe that he could do it, and he wanted to be able to grab a drink anytime he needed one.

During lunch, Joe told Logan the story of the two wolves.

"Long ago, there was a little boy who was afraid of absolutely everything. He was afraid of the dark, he was afraid of loud noises, he was afraid of other kids, and afraid of making mistakes, but the thing he was most afraid of was having others laugh and make fun of him. He became so afraid of everything and everyone that he would do anything he could to avoid being around anyone. Some would even say that he was afraid of his own shadow."

Logan took a drink of water but kept looking at and listening to Joe.

"One day, his grandfather saw him crying and asked gently, 'What's wrong?'

'I'm tired of being afraid of so many things and always trying to run away from them,' the boy said tearfully.

His grandfather patted him on the head and said, 'If you want to overcome your fears and stop being afraid, then you need to stop feeding that wolf.'

'What wolf?' the boy asked, confused.

'The wolf named Fear,' the grandfather replied.

Noticing the confused look on the boy's face, the grandfather sat down next to him and began telling the story of the two wolves that live inside all of us: a good wolf and a bad wolf. The grandfather explained that every day, these two wolves are in a constant battle with one another. They fight every minute of every day for control of our lives. The good wolf's name is Faith. Faith is full of hope and dreams. It's calm, confident, and positive. It believes in itself and is always striving for success and happiness. The other wolf's name is Fear. Fear is the bad wolf. It is full of ugliness and negativity. It's wild, mean, and out of control, and thrives on failure, pain, intimidation, and self-doubt.

Every single day, these two wolves are battling to dominate our lives: some days Faith wins, and other days Fear wins. When we have success, or when we do something nice or good for ourselves or someone else, Faith takes control. However, when we stop believing in ourselves, and when we allow negative thoughts and self-doubt to creep in, then Fear takes control. Day in and day out, the battle rages on inside of us, but only one wolf can win.

'How do I know who wins?' the boy asked.

His grandfather paused and then quietly said, 'The one you feed.'

Joe took a drink of water and paused, waiting for Logan's reply. Logan sat there quietly looking at Joe but didn't say anything. Joe recognized this look, as he'd seen it many times before when he told this story.

"You see, Logan, these two wolves are the exact opposite in every possible way, and they are just as much a part of you as they were for that little boy."

Logan took another bite of his sandwich and thought for a moment, wondering if that little boy was actually his Uncle Joe.

Joe interrupted his thoughts by asking, "So, which wolf do you feed?"

Logan looked down and quietly said, "Fear, most of the time."

Joe nodded then said, "Do you want to know how to feed the good wolf and starve the bad one?"

"Yes please!" Logan replied.

"Then just treat Fear, the bad wolf, like the weeds we dug up last night. Dig up those fears and false beliefs, then confront them and starve them to death by no longer feeding them. Then, be sure to feed Faith, the good wolf, by believing in yourself, staying true to who you are, and always doing your absolute very best at everything you do."

Logan nodded his head several times. "I can do that!"

Joe smiled and said, "Yes, you can!"

They finished their lunches and sat admiring the view and enjoying the beautiful day.

After several minutes, Logan asked, "Uncle Joe, will you tell me how Doug and David's dads bullied you?"

"Sure, Logan, let's pack up, and I'll tell you about it on our way back home."

As they headed back, Joe told Logan about his childhood bullies. "Their names are Bob and Mike. They are brothers who grew up at the same time as your mom and me. Mike, the older brother, was your mom's age, and Bob, the younger brother, was my age. Bob was the one I had the most trouble with. But it always seemed like it was two on one because anytime Bob started something, Mike was there to back him up."

Joe continued, "The two of them ruled the school and were in constant trouble for fighting, stealing, and all kinds of disrespectful behavior. It seemed they were always doing something unruly to impress their abusive dad."

Logan looked up at Joe. "Their dad was a bully too?"

Joe nodded his head. "Like I mentioned earlier, most bullying happens because of what the kids have seen and experienced, and they just continue to carry on the family tradition."

Logan shook his head and said, "That sucks."

Joe nodded his head in agreement. "It is a shame, Logan, but that's what we're dealing with."

Logan stopped walking and used his stick to knock a broken tree branch into the woods. "You know, Uncle Joe, yesterday when you said that they were jealous of me? I really didn't know what to think. I didn't think that could be true. But now, after hearing about their home life, maybe it is."

On the hike back home, Joe and Logan stopped several times to check out some of the cool things they missed the first time through. Logan grabbed a low tree branch and swung himself up and then jumped back onto the trail. A while later, he noticed a snakeskin on the side of the trail and used his stick to pick it up and investigate it before flinging it into the woods.

Joe shared stories about when he was a kid and how he would sometimes get in trouble for not doing his chores properly. He said that his dad, Logan's grandpa, was a military man who had very strict rules and high expectations. Often, Joe didn't live up to those expectations and found himself getting in trouble.

Joe also told a story about the time he "accidentally" forgot to clean the horse stalls and missed going out on a date because he had to stay home on a Friday night and clean the stalls. Logan and Joe both laughed at the thought of Joe missing a date to shovel horse poop.

Within a few minutes, they came around the bend. "I can see the house from here," Logan said, tiredly.

"Race you to the front porch," Joe challenged, acting like he was taking off.

"Wait, no fair, I've got this backpack on," Logan said as he threw his stick to the ground.

Joe looked at Logan and made an "oh well" gesture with his hands and face, taking a couple of steps before he stopped. "I'm just teasing. I'll take the backpack."

"I got you this time, Uncle Joe," Logan yelled back over his shoulder, dropping the backpack while running as fast as he could.

"No, you don't," Joe said as he threw the backpack over his shoulder without missing a step.

Joe lagged a little but was coming up fast. "I'm catching you; you better hurry up," he said as he got closer to Logan.

"No way!" Logan panted, but he didn't look back.

Joe had closed the gap and was right up next to Logan. They were now neck and neck. Suddenly, Joe took a slight lead, but unlike yesterday, Logan's determination was getting stronger, and he never let up.

"You better hurry, or I'm going to win," Joe said when he was just a few feet from the porch.

With one last burst of speed at the very last second, Logan ran past Joe and past the porch. "I got you, Uncle Joe. I beat you," Logan said, excited and proud of himself.

Joe grinned. "I don't know. That was a close one."

Logan, breathing hard but smiling ear to ear, said, "No, I got you, I won this time."

Molly was sitting on her favorite porch swing as the boys came flying up.

"Mom, did you see it? I won right?" Logan asked.

"I saw it, Logan, and it was close, but ..." Molly paused and kept Logan in suspense for a couple more seconds and then with a huge smile and a lot of excitement, said, "Yes, Logan, you won, you beat your Uncle Joe. You're the champion."

Logan continued smiling as he walked over to his Uncle

Joe and said, "Good race," putting his hand up for a high five.

Joe gave Logan a high five and said, "Good race, but I think I need to see the replay."

Joe grabbed Logan and wrestled around with him a bit, getting him in a headlock and ruffling up his hair before letting him go.

"I'm proud of you, Logan. You didn't give up. I pressured you and pushed you, and you never gave up. Especially at the end when I passed you, you could've just given up, but you didn't, you found it in yourself to dig deeper, and you passed me at the last second. Great job, buddy."

"Thanks, Uncle Joe," Logan replied, still smiling.

"So, what do you think was different today from yesterday?" Joe asked.

"I don't know, I just didn't want to lose. I guess I thought about the two wolves and decided that I didn't want to feed the bad wolf."

"That's awesome," Joe replied, holding his hand out for another high five.

They walked up the steps to the front porch and collapsed into chairs. Joe grabbed a bottle of water from their backpack and tossed it to Logan.

"Did you boys have fun?" Molly asked.

"We had a great time, Mom!" Logan panted.

"Awesome. Well, I can't wait to hear about it," Molly said. "Go ahead and catch your breath and get the animals fed, and you can tell me all about it during dinner."

"Will you help me, Uncle Joe?" Logan asked as he stood

up.

"Wow, first you take me on an all-day hike, and then you beat me in a race, and now you want me to help you do your chores. What's next?" Joe said, smiling as he acted like he could barely get out of the chair.

Logan walked over and pretended to help Joe out of his chair. "Here, let me help you."

They both laughed as they walked to the barn.

Inside the barn, Joe grabbed a rake and a shovel and headed to one of the stalls. "Let's go ahead and grab the wheelbarrow, and I'll help you clean out these stalls. We can work together and get it done twice as fast, and then I can show you a few exercises that I used to do in the barn."

"That sounds great," Logan answered as he grabbed the wheelbarrow.

Joe and Logan worked for the next hour, raking and shoveling the soiled bedding then taking turns hauling the heavy wheelbarrow out to the field to dump it. After they finished cleaning the horse stalls, Logan went over to the water spigot and turned on the hose to fill up the water trough as he always did.

"Hey Logan, hold tight for a second. Do you have a couple of five-gallon buckets?" Joe asked.

"I think so," Logan replied.

"Good, can you grab them for me?"

"Okay," Logan said as he went to find two buckets. "Here they are. What do you need them for?" Logan asked.

"Oh, a little workout that I used to do," Joe said as he

took the buckets from Logan.

"Okay," Logan said hesitantly.

Joe grabbed the hose and began filling up one of the buckets. "Instead of just filling the water trough with the hose, I'd fill the buckets and then carry them one at a time to fill up the water trough."

"Why would you do that?" Logan asked with a confused look on his face. "It's easier with the hose."

"Yes, it's a lot easier with the hose, but I always tried to find ways to exercise in the barn, and this was one of them. In the winter, when the hose might freeze, I'd have to do it this way."

When the first bucket was full, Joe carried it by the handle to the water trough and dumped the water in while the other bucket was filling up. They took turns carrying the buckets until the trough was full. Then they got down five bales of hay and fed the horses and cows.

"Whew, that was a workout," Logan said as he wiped his face with his shirt.

"Oh, we're not done yet," Joe said, grinning.

"But that's all my chores," Logan replied.

"Yes, that's all the chores, but I've got a few exercises for you to help build your muscles and your confidence," Joe said as he climbed the hay bales to the top of the barn. Then Joe jumped up, grabbed one of the rafters, and effortlessly did twenty pull-ups.

"Have you ever done this, Logan?" Joe asked as he hopped down from the rafter.

"Sometimes."

"How many can you do?" Joe asked.

"I'm not sure," Logan replied.

"Well, get up here and let's see." Joe motioned for Logan to hop up and grab the rafter.

Logan jumped up, grabbed a rafter, and did ten pull-ups, and then jumped down.

"Nice job, Logan. Those were ten amazing pull-ups," Joe said.

Logan dusted his hands off on his pants and replied, "Thank you."

Joe jumped back up to the rafters, did another twenty pull-ups, and then said, "Okay, Logan, your turn."

Logan sighed and said, "My arms are tired from carrying the water and the full wheelbarrow loads. I don't think I can do anymore."

"I believe in you, Logan, just do your best," Joe said, persuading Logan to try.

Logan hopped up to the rafters again and halfheartedly did three more pull-ups before hopping down.

"Is that truly all you've got?" Joe asked as he looked directly at Logan.

"Well, if I wasn't so tired, I could probably do more," Logan quietly replied.

"Logan, I want you to remember these two words: attitude and effort. These are two of the most important concepts to achieving anything in life."

"Attitude and effort?" Logan repeated with uncertainty

in his voice.

"Yes, attitude and effort. Your attitude toward doing anything is the fuel for your mind, and then your best effort is what builds your self-worth and self-respect." Uncle Joe continued in a serious voice, "Once you get in the habit of always having the right attitude, and then applying the right amount of effort, that's when your self-confidence really begins to grow. Remember, self-confidence is the number-one key to believing in yourself and is the first step toward becoming bully proof."

"Okay, I'll try again," Logan said. He jumped back up on the rafter and forced himself to do five more pull-ups before hopping down.

"I'm sorry, Uncle Joe, I'm just really tired," Logan said with his head down.

"That's a good start, Logan, but I want you to do this. I want you to say out loud, 'I am going to do five more pull-ups.'"

Logan looked at Joe with defeat in his eyes and mumbled, "I am going to do five more."

Joe reminded Logan again that having the right attitude is extremely important and that attitude is greatly impacted by the confident tone of your voice.

Logan hopped back up on the rafter, struggling greatly, but did five more pull-ups. "I'm sorry, Uncle Joe," Logan said with his head down. He was ashamed of himself.

"Hey, lift your head up. You did five more than you thought you could. I'm proud of you," Joe said as he patted

Logan on the back.

"So you're not mad at me?" Logan asked.

"No, I'm not mad at you. You pushed yourself further than you thought you could, and once you develop the habit of always pushing yourself to do more, then your attitude and effort will take care of themselves."

"Thank you, Uncle Joe," Logan said as he lifted his head up and looked directly at him. It was hard to believe, but another full day had come and gone, and little by little, Logan's confidence was growing.

The next morning, they went to work on the big barn door. Logan grabbed a pry-bar and a hammer and started removing the first rotted board. After struggling for several minutes, Logan looked over at Joe and said, "Do you wanna do this?"

"Nope! I can't let you give up. Remember what I told you about having the right attitude."

Logan nodded his head yes and kept working on the board, thinking that this was harder than he thought it was going to be.

"Good. Now I want you to say, 'I'm going to do this.'"

Logan looked down to the ground and halfheartedly said, "I'm going to try to do this." And he tried again, but the board didn't budge. Logan looked back over to Joe, but Joe just stood there and didn't offer to help. He wanted to see if Logan was going to dig deeper inside himself or just give up.

After several more attempts, Joe tapped Logan on the

shoulder and said, "I want you to realize that there is a huge difference between the words 'try' and 'do.' When you say you're going to try to do something, you really haven't fully committed to it because if it doesn't work, you can always say, 'well, at least I tried.' However, when you say, 'I'm going to do this,' then you have fully committed to keep doing it until you get it done, regardless of how many times it takes. Saying you're going to 'do it' is a declaration to yourself that you won't give up. That's the difference between 'try' and 'do,' and that's the difference between having the right attitude and effort and succeeding and having the wrong attitude and effort and giving up."

Logan nodded his head, looked Joe in the eyes, and proudly said, "I'm going to pry these boards off, and I'm not going to give up."

Joe beamed at Logan. "Now that's the attitude I'm talking about!"

Logan tried three more times. Each time, the pry-bar slipped out from underneath the board. He was clearly getting frustrated and, judging by his body language, he wanted Joe to take over. Joe didn't say a word; he just watched Logan continue to battle with this one board on the massive barn door.

This was a test to see how much grit and determination Logan had. More importantly, Joe wanted Logan to overcome the will to give up and then reap the reward of battling through and accomplishing the goal on his own.

Logan looked at Joe again, almost pleading for him to

take over.

"You've got this, Logan," he said. "Stay focused so the bar doesn't pop out."

Logan grunted again, even louder this time, and CRAAACCKKK. The board started to pull away from the door and, with one more tug, the board broke free and fell to the ground.

"YES! I DID IT!" Logan yelled.

"Yes, you did. I'm so proud of you for not quitting," his uncle replied with a big high five.

Logan hadn't noticed, but his mom had made her way out to where they were working, just in time to see the board fall to the ground.

"That's it, buddy. Great job," Molly said as she handed Joe a big glass of ice water and then walked over to Logan and handed him one too. "I figured you guys were working up a thirst out here."

"Thank you, Molly," Joe said.

"Yeah, thanks Mom," Logan said.

"So how many of those boards have to come off?" Molly asked.

"At least four of them," Joe said. "Maybe more. We'll have to see after we get these off."

Logan took a big drink of water and then wiped the sweat from his forehead. "Wow, that was tough."

"Yes it was, Logan, and you did it because you made a commitment to yourself, and you didn't give up."

"Yes, I did," Logan said as he looked down at the big

board laying on the ground.

"So, how do you feel?" Joe asked.

"Proud of myself," Logan replied.

"Do you think you would feel this way if you would've given up?"

"No, probably not."

"That's the difference between try and do," Joe told him.

As Joe watched Logan finish pulling the rest of the old boards off the barn, he reminded Logan that his attitude toward doing anything is what fueled his mind and helped push him to put forth his best effort. Logan and Joe talked about being aware of the negative self-talk. How saying words like "I can't," I'm not strong enough," "I'm not good enough," or "I'm not smart enough" are very destructive words and are essentially planting negative weeds in his mind's garden.

Joe could tell that these lessons, the positive seeds, were starting to take hold in Logan's mind.

CHAPTER 6

ON THE WAY TO THE STORE, after singing along to a couple of 1980s rock songs, Joe praised Logan for his attitude and effort, especially his commitment to getting the boards off the barn door and not giving up.

Logan loved hearing this from his uncle. He felt a bond forming between them, and it helped him open up about everything he was going through.

He told Joe how much he loved hockey and how grateful he was that Joe was helping him become bully proof so he could stand up to Doug and David. Logan talked about how much he enjoyed the hike yesterday and that he liked the story of the two wolves. He said he was going to work even harder on his attitude and effort so he could do more pull-ups and get stronger.

Joe listened intently as Logan talked the entire way. It was obvious that the lessons and accomplishments from the past two days had boosted Logan's spirits.

They entered the store, and Logan spotted a large cart. "There's the cart we need for the lumber," he said as he hurried ahead of Joe to get it. Just as he grabbed the cart and began backing it out of the aisle, he stopped. The smile he had just seconds ago had turned into a look of terror.

"Well, well, well, what do we have here?" asked Doug in an intimidating tone.

"It looks like a crybaby, wannabe hockey player to me," David responded, laughing.

It was Doug and David, and they were standing directly in front of Logan. They had seen him when he came into the store and devised a plan to scare him. Logan, in all his excitement, hadn't seen them, and now he was face to face with his bullies. He was alone and several aisles ahead of Joe because he had rushed ahead to grab the cart.

Logan couldn't move as all the terrifying images of what these two had done to him over the years flooded his mind. In an instant, all his previous joy and excitement had disappeared. He went from being talkative, happy, and excited to the timid little boy who had become the victim of this endless harassment. The confidence he had earlier in the day was gone. Doug and David, sensing his fear like sharks smelling blood in the water, attacked.

The few seconds it took for Joe to walk up seemed like forever. Being frozen with fear caused Logan's mind and body to panic and turned the seconds into hours.

Joe, who was standing out of sight, watched the whole thing to see how Logan would respond. But as soon as he saw Logan put his head down in defeat, and then saw Doug try to ram the cart into Logan's stomach, Joe walked up to them.

"What's going on boys?" he asked in a polite but firm tone. The power in his voice and his commanding presence startled Doug and David.

No one said a word as Logan's head and shoulders slumped further forward in a clearly defeated posture.

"Who are your friends, Logan?" Joe asked.

"We're not his friends!" David said disrespectfully.

"Yeah, we're not friends with loser crybabies," Doug chimed in.

"Then why are you bothering him?" Joe asked firmly.

Doug and David struggled to find something cool to say. They weren't used to people, even adults, standing up to them. The boys were surprised that someone who looked like Joe was with Logan.

"Doug, David, where are you?" The silence was broken when Bob, Doug's dad and David's uncle, called out, "You were supposed to get a cart and meet me in the lumber aisle. What are you doing?"

"I'm over here, Dad, I just got a cart," Doug said as he yanked the cart from Logan's grip.

Logan didn't resist. He freely let go of the cart, never lifting his head to look at them.

By now, Bob had walked over to where the boys were and saw Logan standing there with his head down. He noticed Joe, but he didn't recognize him. Then Bob did what all "wannabe tough guys" do when they see another man they don't know. He looked Joe up and down, looking for a weakness.

Joe was wearing blue jeans and a black T-shirt that showed off his muscular arms and chest. Bob was a thick, stocky man, about six feet tall with big arms but was clearly out of shape. He had on a black baseball hat with the words "Afraid? You Better Be!" in big white letters on the front. He had a cocky manner that was meant to intimidate anyone who would dare threaten his manliness.

There were a few seconds of awkward silence as Bob looked over Joe, trying to figure out if he knew him or not.

Joe calmly stood next to Logan and looked directly at Bob.

"What's going on over here? Is this little pipsqueak giving you boys trouble?" Bob asked arrogantly as he looked at his boys and then back at Joe to see if he had intimidated him.

Bob may not have recognized Joe, but Joe sure recognized Bob. This was the guy, along with his brother Mike, who had bullied Joe almost every single day when he was younger. Joe's mind wandered back to the countless times they had bullied him, including the time when he actually got into a fight with Bob at hockey practice.

Joe now knew that what had happened that night was a culmination of years of bullying, combined with the fear of previously losing control and really hurting someone. His mind flashed back to that night ...

Practice had started off as normal, with Bob and Mike taking turns hitting Joe with their sticks when the coach wasn't looking, but this time, Bob decided to take things further and, without warning, he skated up behind Joe and gave him a hard two-hand slash with his stick across the back of Joe's legs. Joe fell to the ice, and Bob jumped on top of him and started hitting him. The coach rushed over and pulled Bob off Joe, and then to Joe's surprise, the coach told all the players to make a circle and for Bob and Joe to throw out their sticks and then get in the middle of the circle and fight it out.

Joe hesitated. He couldn't believe what was happening. Bob took advantage of his hesitation, punching Joe in the face, knocking him to the ice. Joe managed to wrestle on top of Bob and started punching Bob in the face over and over. They were wearing helmets with full face shields and their hockey gloves, and the face shields were taking the majority of the impact, so neither one of them was in any danger of getting badly hurt.

The coach wanted to help Joe overcome his fears and stand up for himself. Even though Joe ended up on top and clearly landed more punches than Bob did, he was holding back as he started punching Bob. He was afraid of completely losing control again like he had when he hurt that bigger kid on the playground.

Everyone, including the coach, thought that Joe had finally defeated his archnemesis, but Joe was more scared than ever. He knew that he didn't do enough to scare Bob, but he did make Bob look bad in front of others, and that meant that Bob and Mike were going to get even.

For a long time after that day, Joe wished that he hadn't fought back and had just let Bob beat him up, because for the next several years, Bob and Mike made it their personal mission to abuse Joe every time they could.

One of the worst things about being repeatedly bullied and not standing up for yourself is that you become an easy target for everyone. The longer it goes on, the worse it gets. Eventually, this led to Joe having anxiety, depression, and severe anger management issues, which took him years to get over.

Now, here he was, face to face with one of his childhood bullies. But, things were a lot different now. Joe was no longer that scared, skinny kid that Bob and Mike used to beat up; he was in incredible physical shape. He was a Seventh Degree Black Belt and Master Martial Arts Instructor and made a living teaching hand-to-hand combat and self-defense strategies. He had spent the last three decades traveling all over the world, training with some of the best martial artists.

Joe was much more confident now than the last time he and Bob had met. But Bob was pretty much the same bully he was thirty years ago.

"Who are you supposed to be, Logan's new daddy?" Bob rudely interrupted Joe's thoughts.

"No ... I'm his uncle," Joe confidently responded.

"His uncle?" Bob paused as a confused look came over his face. He looked at Joe again, this time looking more closely at his face.

"Ah ... I should've recognized you. You're Little Joe?" Bob said, laughing as he looked back to Doug and David for their validation. "Wait until I tell Mike that Little Joe is back in town. Oh, he's going to love hearing this. Little Joe the karate boy is back!"

"Boys, this is Little Joe. Me and Mike used to whoop up on him when he was your age. It's kinda funny that you two are doing the same thing to his nephew. I guess being a wimp runs in the family." Bob was laughing and added, "So, what, are you here to protect this little pipsqueak from my boys?"

Logan was clearly nervous when Joe casually turned to him and said, "It looks like this cart is taken, so let's grab another one."

"That's right, you better grab another cart!" Bob said, taking an aggressive step toward Joe.

Joe didn't move; he just looked directly into Bob's eyes. Something about Joe's posture and the look in his eyes told Bob that it would probably be smart to stop right where he was. He stopped immediately. While the look on Bob's face showed his fear, he quickly tried to collect himself, hoping that Doug and David hadn't noticed.

Another few seconds passed and then Bob boldly said, "Well, you may have put on some fake muscles, but underneath, you're still that skinny little kid I used to beat up.

You better watch it if you know what's good for you."

Bob pushed his chest out, trying to look tough while he grabbed the cart and made a threatening motion as if he was going to run over Joe. Then he laughed and headed down the aisle.

"Who was that?" Doug asked, running to catch up.

Joe casually looked over at Logan and winked. "What do you say we get another cart? I think that one had a bad wheel anyway."

Logan tried to answer and act normal, but he was still feeling scared and in shock at what had just happened. All he could do was nod.

He wondered, *How could Joe be so calm and even crack a joke after what just happened?*

Joe and Logan finished getting their supplies and headed to the checkout. Joe had noticed that Bob and the boys were watching them in every aisle, and although he didn't look directly at them, he still knew where they were. So, he wasn't surprised when Bob and the boys rushed up and cut in front of them.

"We were here first!" Bob sneered as he attempted to ram his cart into Joe's.

At the last moment, Joe moved, allowing Bob to ram his cart into the side of the checkout lane. The crash made a loud bang, and everyone standing around stopped and looked their way.

"Yeah, we were here first, wait your turn," Doug said, looking directly at Logan.

"Losers," David mouthed as all three of them cut in front of Joe and Logan.

Joe didn't say a word; he simply backed the cart up and went to another checkout lane. They could hear Bob and the boys laughing and celebrating their apparent victory.

Logan had thought he was gaining some confidence over the past couple of days working with Joe, but when Doug and David jumped out and surprised him, he still became frozen and overwhelmed with fear. He wondered if he would ever have enough confidence to stand up to them by himself.

"They're only barking dogs seeking attention. Just ignore them," Joe said, trying to help Logan relax.

Logan nodded his head but didn't say anything.

"You okay, Logan?" Joe asked.

"I'm fine, I guess, but aren't you going to do anything?"

"What would you like me to do?"

"I don't know ... a karate kick to the face maybe." Logan tried to make a joke, but it was exactly what he'd like to see his Uncle Joe do.

"Yes, that's what I should've done," Joe said as he looked up to the ceiling, giving a look like, *Why didn't I think of that?*

Logan was surprised by this comment. "Really?"

Joe slowly shook his head side to side. "Some things aren't worth my time. You'll learn this lesson soon enough. So do you want a tea or a soda?" Joe said as he opened the mini fridge door by the checkout stand.

"What ...?" Logan said, trying to collect his thoughts.

"Do you want a tea or a soda?" Joe asked again.

"Ah ... I'll take a soda. Please."

CHAPTER 7

AFTER LOADING THE LUMBER and supplies into the back of Joe's truck, Logan climbed in the front seat while Joe returned the cart. Logan was relieved when Joe got in the truck because he was nervous wondering if Bob might try and sneak up behind them.

"Are you upset with me?" Logan asked while looking out the window.

"Upset with you? Of course not, Logan. Why in the world would I be upset with you?"

"Because I froze. I just stood there letting them pick on me again."

"Yeah, I guess you should've jumped up and kicked all three of them in the face with a jump side kick. That would've probably been the right thing to do." Joe glanced Logan's way with a smirk.

"That would've been cool! Can you teach me to do that?" Logan laughed.

"Actually, I can. But first I must teach you to believe in yourself and how to block out negative words and comments from people who don't matter."

Logan started to think about that when Joe interrupted with, "So, what do you say we grab some lunch before we head back home?"

"Okay, that sounds good," Logan replied.

"Well, let's call your mom and see if she wants to meet us somewhere."

"Okay." Logan nodded his head in agreement.

After getting off the phone, Joe turned to Logan. "Your mom said there's a nice little deli about ten minutes from here. She told me that you're a huge fan of their meatball sub."

"The Deli. Yes, they've got the best meatball subs anywhere," Logan said as a small smile resurfaced on his face.

"There's your smile, Logan. I wondered what happened to it," Joe said as he flipped on his right turn signal.

"Uncle Joe, did you ever get into a fight with either Bob or Mike?"

Joe paused and then answered. "We had several encounters, and most of the time, it was both of them against me, so I rarely did much of anything to defend myself. I just took their abuse. They would punch and kick me in the locker room, and on the ice, they hit me in the back of the legs with their sticks when coach wasn't looking."

Logan sat there quietly looking at Joe.

"But there was one time during practice when I did get into a fight with Bob, well, truthfully, it was more of a wrestling match on the ice."

Joe told Logan about his fight with Bob, the fight he was just thinking about in the hardware store.

Logan smiled, and then he paused and sighed deeply. "I'm glad that you're here with me. Thanks for helping me," Logan, who was truly grateful, said with sincerity in his voice.

"I'm glad, too, Logan. It's been too long since I've seen you."

"Where have you been the last few years?" Logan asked.

"I've been traveling the country, teaching self-defense and hand-to-hand combat techniques. I've also been conducting seminars and giving speeches to kids, adults, and parent groups on the ABCs to becoming bully proof. To be honest, I guess I just lost track of time."

Joe continued, "I'm a little ashamed of myself for not checking in on you more often. Here I am empowering thousands of kids, parents, and adults on how to protect themselves and how to become bully proof, and I wasn't here to help my own sister and her amazing son. I teach people to be aware of their surroundings, but I wasn't aware of my only family."

Logan shifted in his seat and looked back at Joe. "It's okay, Uncle Joe, I understand."

There was a brief moment of silence between the two of them, with only the radio in the background and the sound of Joe's truck tires humming along on the highway.

Within minutes, they were pulling into The Deli. Molly had already arrived and was standing by the front door when they walked in.

"Hey boys, did you get everything you need from the store?"

"We did, and we ran into some old friends," Joe said as he leaned over and patted Logan on the back.

"You did? Who?" Molly asked expectantly.

"Well, I got to meet Doug and David, and I also got to see Bob."

"Oh," Molly sighed, now showing her nervousness.

"Yes, and I can see that Bob hasn't changed, and as for Doug and David, those apples didn't fall far from the tree."

"I'm afraid that Bob and Mike are raising their boys to be just like them, and it's making everyone's life on the hockey team miserable," Molly replied.

"Well, I'm glad I'm back in town. After we finish these amazing sandwiches, Logan and I are going to ramp up our training," Joe said and then took a bite of his sub sandwich.

"Why, did something happen?" Molly asked.

Joe looked over at Logan. "Do you want to tell your mom?" he asked.

Molly's eyes widened as she looked directly at Logan. "Logan, are you okay?"

"Yeah, I'm fine, Mom, it's ... it's just that I thought I

was getting more confident, but when they snuck up and surprised me, I was scared."

Logan told his mom about the entire event, and just as Molly and Joe finished eating, an almost magical thing happened. Suddenly, a huge smile brightened up Logan's face as he had an amazing thought.

"You know what? I gave them too much power. I let them get in my mind, just like a weed in the garden. I gave them the power because I didn't believe in myself. I fed the wrong wolf," Logan confidently said.

"So, what do you think we should do about this?" Joe asked Logan.

"Keep building my self-confidence and self-respect," Logan replied.

"That sounds like a great idea," Joe said and continued, "You know, confidence is such a fragile thing, especially at the beginning, and even more so after it's been destroyed. But one thing's for sure: once it starts growing through hard work, good habits, plus the right attitude and effort, it will become stronger than the biggest oak tree. And, do you know what an oak tree starts out as?"

"A seed?" Logan said, almost questioning himself.

"Yes, that's exactly right. Just look at all those amazing trees," Joe said, pointing out the window of the deli toward the park across the street. "Each one of those huge, strong oak trees was once a little acorn that had the determination to grow into the massive tree it was meant to be. So how about you, Logan? Are you ready to push yourself to the next level?"

"Yes I Am!" Logan said with more confidence than Molly had ever heard from him.

"Great. Let's finish up lunch and get back to the farm and back to training," Joe said as he wiped his face with a napkin.

"It sounds like you two have a plan. I'm going to head to the store, and I'll see you at home later," Molly said as she gave Logan a kiss on the cheek and headed to her car.

During the drive home, a popular song popped on the radio, and Joe turned it up and started singing along. Logan looked over at him.

"Do you know this song, Logan?"

"I think I've heard it before."

"The name of the song is "I Won't Back Down" by Tom Petty. That's kind of cool hearing this song after what we just talked about and what happened in the hardware store," Joe said and then continued singing with the radio.

"Can I ask you something?"

"Sure, Logan, what's on your mind?" Joe asked as he sang the next line to the song and then flipped on the left blinker to turn down the lane to Logan's house.

"Were you scared when Bob started coming toward you? I mean, he's taller than you and a lot bigger than you. Were you scared?"

Joe shrugged. "Did I seem scared?"

"No, not at all. But were you?"

"The truth is, Logan, I don't remember being scared."

"You don't remember if you were scared or not? I know I was scared," Logan responded.

"Logan, there are a lot of things that scare me, but I always remind myself to feed the right wolf by staying calm, keeping a clear head, believing in myself, and having faith in my abilities."

"Do you think I will get there?" Logan asked.

"Get where?" Joe said as he winked at Logan.

"You know, as confident as you are?"

Joe pulled into the driveway and then backed up his truck directly in front of the barn door.

"Logan, I know you can. But it doesn't matter what I think. Confidence is something you must earn for yourself by believing in yourself. And I promise you, I'm going to do everything within my power to help you. But you must be the one, and it starts with feeding the right wolf."

The next morning, Joe was up early and repeated his morning workout, including feeding the animals again. As Joe came inside, Logan was making his way downstairs, and Molly had just finished making her famous pancakes. The amazing smell wafted throughout the house from the kitchen.

"I hope you boys are hungry," she said as she set the plate of steaming hot pancakes on the table.

"These smell amazing, Mom."

"Thank you, Logan," Molly said as she kissed him on the forehead.

"My mom's pancakes are the best! I like mine with chocolate chips," Logan said while turning toward Joe.

"Yes, they do look and smell delicious," Joe said as he washed his hands in the kitchen sink.

After breakfast, they sat around the table, and Joe talked about the ABCs to become bully proof. He said the reason he wanted Logan to learn about digging up weeds and planting the right seeds and working hard to develop the right attitude and effort before discussing the ABCs was that he wanted the garden in Logan's mind to be ready for those seeds to be planted.

"Logan, do you think that all bullies are bad people?"

Logan quickly nodded his head yes.

Joe smiled slightly while slowly nodding his head, mirroring Logan. "I thought the same thing when I was your age, and I've thought it many times as an adult. Most people think of bullies like they are mean, horrible monsters that are too big and too intimidating to stop. In reality, they are just people who choose to do mean, horrible things. And most of the time, it's because someone has done mean, horrible things to them."

"Really?" Logan wasn't sure he agreed with Uncle Joe.

"Or maybe they have been brought up in a bullying household, and that's all they know. They think that putting others down or hurting someone else will help them feel better about themselves. Of course, we know this isn't true; the pain they cause others only causes more pain inside themselves."

"Okay, but ..." Logan said and then stopped.

"I get it, Logan. I just want you to realize that Doug and David are kids. They are not giant monsters. They are living, breathing, emotional human beings, which means they have feelings, and they also experience pain. And, from what I know about their dads, they have grown up in a bullying household. In no way does this justify their behavior or make it okay to treat you and others this way. Their behavior is completely unacceptable, and they deserve severe consequences for their actions. That, however, does not give you the right to walk up and punch them in the face. Remember, this would make you no better than them."

Joe paused as he saw the look on Logan's face, the same look he'd seen thousands of times before when he talked about this. The look that says, *After all they have done to me, I feel like it does give me the right.*

"I get it, Logan, and I know personally how you're feeling. Many times, I thought the same thing: that bullies deserve to have their butts kicked for everything they've done to hurt people. But my goal is to teach you a better way of handling things so you don't have to go around fighting your entire life. Because the truth is, if fighting is the only thing you learn, then you will never learn to control your anger, and you'll end up becoming no better than the bully yourself."

Joe paused to see if the expression on Logan's face had changed. Logan looked back at Joe with his soft brown eyes and gave a halfhearted smile.

"Thanks," Logan politely replied. "I just want it to stop."

Over the next hour, the three of them sat at the table as Joe dove deep into the ABCs to become bully proof.

"The 'A' stands for awareness to avoid conflict," Joe said. "Always be aware of your surroundings because by being aware, you can avoid most dangerous situations. This also includes bullies on social media. The best way to avoid these bullies is by not accepting people you don't know and by deleting people who are mean, rude, and inappropriate. You also need to know the ways you might be bullying yourself, thinking and saying hurtful things about you and tearing down your self-confidence," he emphasized. "Essentially, the first step to becoming bully proof is in not putting yourself in harm's way whenever it can be avoided." They discussed the locker room and the importance of avoiding being alone with the bullies, developing a buddy system with Logan's friends so they won't leave each other alone but stay until they are all changed and ready instead of leaving individually.

"Awareness and Avoidance is always the very first step. You have to do everything you can to be aware and then avoid any type of conflict, if at all possible, because any time you are involved in a conflict, you could get hurt. Also, today, it doesn't matter who started the fight or who ended the fight; most of the time, both people are considered equally guilty for being involved, especially at school."

Logan remembered when he had tried to stand up for himself by pushing Doug away and how he got in just as much trouble because, in the principal's words, "*You are equally guilty for being involved in the altercation.*"

"That doesn't seem fair, but that's what happens at my school, and that's what happened to me when I tried to protect myself."

"I agree, it isn't fair, but those are the rules that most schools have. It's also a good reminder to try and avoid conflict whenever possible. However, I want to be clear that this step is for avoiding potentially dangerous people, situations, and unnecessary conflict. I am not encouraging you to ever run away from your fears. That's different than being aware and avoiding unnecessary trouble. Being aware of your surroundings is the most vital step to protecting yourself and staying safe. The more you practice awareness, the more aware you'll become of everything going on around you, and the safer you'll be. Just like that pile of horse manure you so gracefully sidestepped yesterday in the field. Without awareness of your surroundings, you would have a stinky mess to clean off your shoes!"

Logan smiled and looked at his mom while nodding his head. "That was a big pile."

Joe continued, "You should always pay attention to where the bully hangs out and avoid that area. For example, if you know they eat lunch at table two, then find a group of friends and sit across the cafeteria at table eleven. You can also ask to have your locker moved so that you're further away from them. Remember to use the buddy system. Try not to be alone in places where you could be cornered by yourself. It's always safer and much more fun to be with friends anyway."

Logan and Molly listened attentively to Joe's suggestions on how to avoid bullies and dangerous situations.

"Things have changed a lot since I was a kid. When I was your age, regardless of how much I was bullied during the day and how rough it was at school, I knew that at 3:15, the bullying would end because school got out," Joe continued. "I got to go home and didn't have to worry about the bullies until the next day. Now, everyone has a cell phone with text messaging and social media accounts. People are able to bully others at any time of the day or night and all weekend."

"That's for sure," Logan said quietly. "I want to keep them from bullying me, but I don't want to have to give up my social media. I don't think that's fair; it's the only way I get to talk to some of my friends on the weekends."

"Logan, you know how to block people and how to work your phone better than your mom and I do, so just block these boys. There is no reason for you to have any communication with them. I know that your mom has temporarily deleted your social media channels. So, we don't have to worry about that for the time being."

Logan nodded his head, showing some frustration.

"Are you upset about this?" Joe asked.

"Sure, a little bit. It doesn't seem fair that I can't have it when I'm not the one doing anything wrong," Logan replied.

"I get it, Logan. If I were your age, I would think the same thing. But first, let's get your confidence built back up and get all those weeds dug out of your mind's garden, and then I'm sure your mom will let you access some of the safer social media channels again. You still need to realize that social media is very powerful and can be dangerous for adults, and even more so for teens. There are people on social media who have extremely bad intentions. They trick kids and adults into doing things and saying things they normally wouldn't. They even trick kids into meeting them places without their parents and then try to abduct them. It's scary, Logan, and it happens every single day. That's why I want you to realize just how powerful and how dangerous that phone of yours can be."

"Okay. I understand," Logan quietly replied.

"There's one more part of the 'A,' and that is being aware and avoiding the many ways we can bully ourselves."

"Bully ourselves?" Logan questioned.

"Yes, at times we can be our own worst bully by the negative things we say about ourselves, such as, '*I can't do this*,' '*I'm dumb*,' '*I'm an idiot*,' '*I'm ugly*,' or '*Everyone hates me*.' We also bully ourselves by doing things we know we shouldn't do or by going places we know we shouldn't go, or by hanging around people we shouldn't be around. These are all self-bullying behaviors that we need to be aware of and then avoid doing them because, if we bully ourselves, then we often attract bullying behaviors from others."

"Wait, so, I could be attracting bullies because I've bullied myself?" Logan asked.

"Yes, it's very possible, but even if you don't attract

bullies, you're still bullying yourself by planting negative thoughts in your mind's garden, which is also feeding the bad wolf."

"I don't want to do that," Logan replied.

"No, you don't," Joe said, nodding his head and agreeing with Logan.

"So, that's the 'A,'" Molly said after listening closely to ways she could help Logan use the 'A' to be aware of and avoid potential adult bullies.

"Yes, that's the 'A,' the first step. But, considering how long this bullying has been going on, we may need to move through the steps a little quicker than normal. Logan, I still want you to follow the steps in the correct order to give you indisputable proof that you did absolutely everything you could to avoid physical conflict. The ABCs were put together to stop the bullying before it gets out of hand, but they are also there to protect you in case things do get physical."

CHAPTER 8

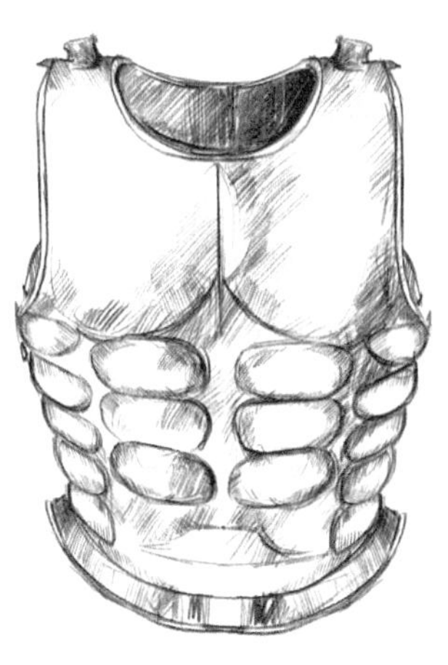

JOE AND LOGAN HEADED OUT to the barn and spent the next couple of hours training before grabbing drinks and sitting on the front porch to rest.

"I've got a question for you, Logan. Would you ever think about going to school without a shirt on?"

"No, of course not," Logan chuckled.

"Really? Huh?" Joe said, acting surprised. "Well, just like you don't go anywhere without a shirt on, from now on, you aren't going to go anywhere without your bully proof armor on."

"My bully proof armor?" Logan asked.

"Yep, that is the 'B' in the ABCs to becoming bully proof. The 'B' stands for believing in yourself by putting on your bully proof armor," Uncle Joe replied. "This is what protects you and keeps you safe from the negative comments and actions of others, and any negative thoughts you have about yourself."

"My bully proof armor," Logan said with a smirk as he looked down at his chest and put his fists on his hips in a classic superhero pose.

"You got it," Joe winked. "Think of it this way: the mean comments that bullies say about you are like poisonous arrows. These arrows hurt and cause a lot of pain because it doesn't feel good when people laugh at you or call you names or exclude you from the group. This armor is your way of mentally blocking these arrows so that they don't pierce you."

"I like that example, Uncle Joe." Logan was nodding his head. "I've never thought of it that way, but it makes a lot of sense."

Joe smiled and continued, "Always remember that the way people treat you isn't about you, it's about them and their own fears and jealousy of you. So, they always attack your two most vulnerable areas. Do you know what those are?"

Logan turned his head and thought for a second. "Your stomach and your nose."

"Well, those are very vulnerable areas, but the most vulnerable areas that bullies attack with their words are our heart and mind. That's why we need to strengthen our bully proof armor to protect our heart from being hurt and protect our mind from negative weeds."

Logan reached down and grabbed his water bottle to take another drink before asking, "So how do I strengthen my armor?"

"That's a great question." Joe took a drink of water, too, before continuing. "The best way to strengthen your bully proof armor is by building your self-confidence through hard work and always pushing yourself to be your very best. When you do this, you will not only gain a tremendous amount of self-respect, but your self-confidence will also grow."

"Attitude and effort," Logan said. "I remember that lesson."

"Of course, you do. You must have the right attitude and effort to dig up any negative thoughts that are in your mind, because your self-confidence can't grow if it is being suffocated by weeds. It's either the seeds we want to grow or the weeds we don't."

Another weeds and garden example, Logan thought to himself and then asked, "So how do I dig these weeds out of my mind?"

Joe asked Logan to run into the house and grab a pen and notebook to write in.

Logan returned a few minutes later. "Will this work?" he asked, showing Joe one of his school notebooks.

"Sure, that will work for the time being, but I want you to get a notebook that is only used for your thoughts, and

I want you to write on the outside of it, 'Logan's Journal of Weeds, Seeds, and Trees.'"

"Okay," Logan said.

Joe continued, "This will be your personal journal for all your thoughts and successes. It will help you get your thoughts out of your mind and on paper so you can see them. Then you can decide which ones you want to keep and which ones you want to get rid of. Think of it like this: you will be separating the weeds and seeds to allow your mind's garden to grow the positive thoughts you want. The trees will be the successes you've had in the past from the positive seeds you've already planted."

"What should I write first?" Logan asked, excited to get started.

"Draw a line down the center of the paper. Good, now at the top, write the word Weeds on the left side of the line and Seeds on the right side of the line." Logan drew out the words as his uncle told him. "Okay now, let's dig up some weeds first. Underline the word Weeds and start writing any negative thoughts below it."

Logan underlined the word Weeds and then paused and looked back up at Joe.

"Just start writing. Write down the first negative, hurtful thought that pops into your head. Maybe write down all the bad names, rude comments, and hurtful things that Doug and David, or any other bully, has done to you. It will be a little difficult at first, just like it was digging up those weeds in the garden, but once you have these out of your mind and on paper, you can look at these weeds and see just how ridiculous and untrue they really are. That's when you're going to wonder why in the world you spent any time at all worrying about them."

Logan started writing and, within seconds, he had a list of names and comments in the Weeds section.

"You're stupid. You're dumb. You suck. You're the worst hockey player. No one likes you. You're a wimp. You're no good. You're not a man. Everyone hates you."

"How's this?" Logan asked as he showed his list to Joe.

"Pretty harsh, but good job writing them down. The next step is to work on your Seeds." Joe pointed at the column. "Underline it, and then write all the positive things that you know to be true about yourself. Write the positive seeds directly across from the weeds that we know are not true, so across from you're stupid, write I am smart." Logan wrote I Am Strong across from the weed that said you're a wimp.

Logan countered as many weeds as he could with positive thoughts, like being fun, a good friend and son, and a hard worker. When he couldn't think of any more, Joe suggested that he write down all the amazing things he had in his life, like his loving mom, his health, his horses, and of course, his awesome uncle ...

Logan smiled and continued writing, and within seconds, he had a long list in the Seeds section.

"Wow. I thought that I had more weeds than seeds, but looking at this paper, I've got twice as many seeds," Logan said, proudly showing his paper to Joe.

Joe patted Logan on the back and laughed to himself because this was the same reaction he got every time he did this drill. "Of course you do, buddy. You are an amazing kid! You know, this is a tool that I also do with adults and professional athletes to help them realize their strengths to become their personal best and strengthen their bully proof armor."

"You mean professional athletes do this same drill?" Logan asked.

"They sure do. Now, you are going to cross out all the weeds and water the seeds so you can grow your trees."

Logan smiled at the thought of him doing the same drill as a professional hockey player.

Joe explained to Logan that he should read each negative comment or negative thought in the Weeds section, and then say to himself, "Not true, not me, no way," and then physically cross it out with his pen. "This is like digging up the weed and taking away its power to grow in your mind."

Next, Logan read each positive comment out loud to affirm its truth. Joe told Logan that affirmations are one of the most powerful ways to start believing in yourself, improve your self-confidence, and strengthen your bully proof armor.

Logan was a little confused at first.

Joe explained, "Think of affirmations as positive thoughts and phrases about yourself that you want to come true. The mind is extremely powerful, and it will believe what you tell it. Just like your garden will grow what you plant in it."

Joe looked over Logan's Seeds list and made a few suggestions that would work great as affirmations. He had Logan write down: I Am Strong, I Believe in Me, I Am Awesome, I Am a Great Hockey Player, I Am Confident, and I Am Bully Proof.

Logan quietly read the affirmations, feeling awkward and lacking confidence and belief in the words he was saying.

Once again, Joe saw a look that he'd seen countless times. He smiled and said, "I get it, Logan. When you do this for the first time, you're probably going to feel foolish and might even laugh at yourself, but that is good too. The smile that follows laughter is a big step to feeling good inside."

Logan nodded his head, showing that he understood. He felt a little more comfortable when he said the affirmations again.

"Good," Joe said. "Now, go inside and find a mirror so you can look directly in your eyes, and say them as confidently as you can. Practice so you get comfortable with it. No one else needs to hear it; this is for you."

Logan walked into the bathroom, shut the door, and stood in front of the mirror. He practiced his affirmations until he could do them without laughing.

When Logan came back outside, Joe reached over and gave him a knuckle pound. "That's a great start, Logan, and there's another positive seed planted in your mind's garden."

"The final section is the Trees. So on the page opposite from the Weeds and Seeds, write the word Trees in the top middle of the page."

Logan wrote Trees and underlined it just as he had with the words on the first page.

Joe continued, "This will be where you write all the successes you've gained from planting the right seeds and from working hard with the right attitude and effort."

Logan scratched his head and then started tapping his pen on his notebook. "I can't think of any trees."

"Sure you can, Logan. Are you a better hockey player now than you were three years ago?"

"Yes," Logan replied.

"In what area?" Joe asked.

"Well, I used to have a hard time skating backward, but now I can do it without any trouble."

"Good, well, write that down. And I'm sure you've got countless other examples of how you're a much better skater and hockey player than you used to be, so be sure to write those down as well."

"Well, I do shoot the puck a lot harder, and I'm a lot faster."

"Good. Be sure to write those down, and when you're finished with that, I want you to write down other areas you've worked hard at. Like taming your horse, Smokey, so you can ride him, and getting an A on that math test you were telling me about."

Logan wrote for several minutes. Before he knew it, he had a huge list under the Trees section. "Man, I never would've thought that I had so many successes, I mean trees," Logan said excitedly.

"That's the power of the journal," Joe said as he looked at Logan's list. "The simple act of getting the thoughts and successes out of your head and on paper is extremely powerful. As long as you're honest with yourself, you will always see that you have far more trees and seeds than you do weeds. But, when the weeds are trapped in your mind, they seem to spiral out of control and appear to be far more and far worse than they really are. Those few weeds will occupy the majority of your mind's garden and suffocate all your seeds and kill all your trees if you let them."

"Wow!" Logan said as he looked down at his list again and then back up at Joe. "I can't believe how true that is. I would've never believed it if I didn't see it."

When Molly got home from work, Logan eagerly showed her his lists. She smiled. She was so proud of

Logan and so grateful to see his confidence growing.

Joe suggested they work together to create a nice, personal weed, seed, and tree journal that Logan could use to continue strengthening his bully proof armor.

"So, is that it for the 'B'?" Logan asked.

"Almost," Joe replied. "But I want to teach you how to play a little game that I call the 'Verbal Bully Proof' game."

"The 'Verbal Bully Proof' game?" Logan asked.

"Yes. This game shows how well your bully proof armor actually works."

"Okay," Logan said, still smiling and reflecting on his Weeds, Seeds and Trees Journal.

"Have you ever heard the little saying, '*I'm rubber and you're glue, whatever you say bounces off me and sticks to you*'?" Joe continued.

Logan snorted and said, "Yeah, we used to say that in kindergarten."

"Well, grade-school kids are pretty smart because that's exactly how your bully proof armor works, and it's how you win the 'Verbal Bully Proof' game. The rules are very simple. If you believe the bully's words and get upset, you lose. But if you block out the negative words and ignore them, you win. The bully has one goal: to gain power over you by getting you upset. If you give them the power and allow their words to upset you, they win. However, if you don't get upset, and you make it clear that their words aren't bothering you, then you win. When you win, the bully loses interest in playing because they're losing. And no one likes to play a game they can't win.

"Man, you make it all sound so easy," Logan replied.

"Everything that is easy was once hard, and every giant oak tree was once a little acorn seed. It will take time, and you will probably have to play their game a few times and actually win it before they realize they can't win, so they stop. But if you do your best, I promise it will get easier, and I promise you'll get better."

"I just want to be as confident as you are, Uncle Joe."

Realizing how much Logan's self-worth had been damaged by the constant bullying and that the scars in his mind were affecting the way he saw himself and the value he placed on himself, Joe thought of another way to reach Logan.

He reached into his wallet and pulled out a crisp, new one-hundred-dollar bill. Logan's eyes lit up as he wondered if the money was for him. But, before he could say anything, Joe asked him, "What's the value of this one-hundred-dollar bill?"

Logan, thinking this was a trick question, answered hesitantly, "One hundred dollars."

"Right. But what if I crinkle it up in my hand and throw it on the ground and stomp all over it?"

Joe crushed the bill in his hand and threw it on the ground and stomped on it with his boots. "What's it worth now?" he asked.

"Still one hundred dollars," Logan replied.

"Okay, but what if I spit on it?" Joe then spit on the bill and stomped on it again.

Logan couldn't believe what he was watching. *Why in the world was Uncle Joe destroying a hundred-dollar bill?*

"How about now? What's it worth?" Joe asked.

Logan was stuck, caught in a trance staring at the hundred-dollar bill. Then he shrugged his shoulders and answered, "It's still a hundred dollars."

Joe began yelling at the money on the ground, saying it was worthless and it was only a penny and couldn't buy anything. Logan shook his head and laughed.

"Are you sure, even after I crinkled it, stomped on it, humiliated it, and spit on it? Are you sure it still has the same value after everything I've done to it?" Joe asked incredulously.

"Sure, it's still a hundred-dollar bill, so it's still worth one hundred dollars," Logan said. His mind was spinning in circles trying to figure out what his uncle was trying to prove.

Joe bent over and picked up the bill. "So, you're telling me that this one-hundred-dollar bill is still worth one hundred dollars even if it doesn't look like it did when I first pulled it out of my wallet."

"Yes!" Logan confidently said.

"Why?" Joe asked.

"Because it doesn't matter what it looks like; its worth doesn't change."

"Exactly! And that's something that I don't want you to ever forget. You're priceless, and your worth doesn't change based on what someone may have said about you or even done to you. Your self-worth is based on the way you see yourself, not on the thoughts and opinions of others who don't know you. A one-hundred-dollar bill will always be worth one hundred dollars, no matter what I do to it or say about it; its worth doesn't change. Just like your worth doesn't change."

The look on Logan's face showed that he understood. "I get it, Uncle Joe, I really do, but I just want to believe it about myself."

Joe walked over and put his hand on Logan's shoulder and said, "You will, Logan, I promise. I know what you're going through because I went through it, too, when I was younger. I know what it's like to sit on the bench and to be told I'm not good enough, or tall enough, or strong enough, or smart enough. I know how horrible it feels to be laughed at, to be made fun of, to be mocked and called names, to be screamed at, spit on, punched, kicked, scratched, and bit. I've been bullied in every way you can imagine, but it still doesn't change my worth because I know I'm a priceless gift from God."

Logan shook his head in disbelief at the thought of this happening to Joe.

Joe continued, "I tell you, I carried a lot of that pain and those feelings of worthlessness around for years, and it led to a lot of suffering that I don't want you to go through."

Logan's eyes filled with tears thinking about these things happening to his Uncle Joe. They were also painful reminders of the things that were happening to him now.

Joe squeezed Logan's shoulder. "Hey, it's all going to work out. You're going to have all the tools that I never had, making you bully proof, plus an awesome uncle who's going to be here to help when you need it."

Logan looked up and smiled. "Thank you, Uncle Joe. You are pretty awesome."

"You darn right I'm pretty awesome," Joe said as he got Logan in a headlock and wrestled around with him as they headed out to the yard to play some catch before supper.

CHAPTER 9

AFTER FINISHING THE MORNING CHORES and a workout in the barn the next morning, Joe took Logan to the batting cages and then to a family arcade center, where they played arcade games for hours.

On the way home, Logan bragged about beating Joe at air hockey and then thanked him.

"All right, air hockey champ, let's dive into the 'C' of the ABCs to become bully proof."

"Sounds great," Logan said with energy in his voice.

"Let's say that you've tried to avoid the bully, and then you've tried to block out the negative comments with your bully proof armor, and that hasn't worked to stop it. Then the next step is using the 'C,' which stands for communicating clearly and confidently. This is done in two stages. First, you're going to calmly and confidently ask the bully to stop, and then walk away. If the bully doesn't stop, then you report what's going on to a teacher, parent, or trusted adult, telling them exactly what happened and exactly what you would like help with. It is very important that you say clearly what you want help with. If it sounds like you're whining or tattling, you probably won't be taken seriously because they hear whining and tattling all day long. So, you need to clearly tell them what the bully did and what you have done to stop it. Tell them that you tried to avoid the bully, you tried to block out the bully's comments, you have asked the bully to stop, and none of that has worked, so now you are coming to them for help."

"But won't that make it worse if I tattle on them?" Logan asked.

"I want you to realize that when you communicate clearly, you're asking for help because everything you've tried on your own hasn't worked. There is a huge difference between tattling, which is just trying to get someone in trouble, and communicating, where you're asking for help to protect yourself or someone else from harm."

Logan looked out the window of the truck. Joe could see Logan's reflection and knew what Logan was thinking.

"I get it, Logan. At your age, if you go to a teacher, it's going to seem like you're tattling, but this is an important step that shows that you did absolutely everything you could, including asking for help, to stop the bully before it gets worse."

"What if it doesn't work and the bully knows I told on him?"

"Well, that's when you have to move on to the second stage of 'Communicating Clearly.' This will either put a stop to the bullying because you confidently stood up for yourself, or it could escalate the situation. Unfortunately, considering how long Doug and David have been bullying you and that they've already gotten physical and continue to get more physical, there's a good chance that we will have to use the 'D' to stop the bullying. But, I want you to learn and use the ABCs first to show that you did everything you could to avoid the conflict. Learning the ABCs will prevent most future bullying incidents from ever reaching the point they are at now."

Logan looked over at Joe as they turned down the lane toward the farm.

"Yeah, that's what I've been thinking, and that's why I asked if you would teach me how to fight. Because I don't know if anything else is going to stop them."

"I'm not going to lie to you, Logan. Considering how long it's gone on, it may very well come to that. I just want you to know that you will be trained for any situation regardless of what happens, and more importantly, you will have all the tools you need to stop the bullying and become bully proof."

"All right," Logan said, convinced by the confidence in his uncle's words.

Joe pulled up to the barn and signaled for Logan to come over to his side of the truck. "The second stage of communicating clearly is to communicate with courage and confidence by having a strong, defensive posture and using your tiger's eyes and lion's voice."

"Tiger's eyes and lion's voice?"

"Yes, communicating with the intensity of a tiger's eyes and strength of a lion's voice. Because body language is so important in communication. Think of a tiger or a lion. Do you think they are confident?"

"Absolutely. Just look at 'em," Logan replied.

"What makes you think they're confident?" Joe asked.

"Well, the way they look and the way they act. They don't seem to be afraid of anything."

"That's exactly right. Everything about them projects strength and courage, from their posture to the intense look in their eyes and their furious roar. It all displays confidence."

"It does," Logan agreed.

"Imagine a lion, the king of the jungle, being too afraid to make eye contact and too afraid to use its roar, so it walks around whining with its head down and its shoulders slumped forward in a defeated posture. Can you picture this in your mind?"

Logan chuckled. "Not really. A big, ferocious lion walking around whining and looking scared?"

Joe smiled. "That is hard to imagine, isn't it?"

"It sure is," Logan said, laughing at the image in his mind.

"Do you think that if the other animals saw this display of weakness, they would try to take advantage of it?"

"Sure, they would," Logan confidently replied.

"Do you think the same is true for humans? Do you think our posture and body language communicate a lot about our confidence?" Joe asked.

"I guess so."

"Let's test it," Joe said as he put his head down and let his shoulders slouch forward.

"Logan, do I look very confident?"

"No," Logan answered.

"Why not?"

"I don't know, I mean you're still big and muscular, but with your head down and your back hunched down, you just don't look very confident."

Joe looked into the side mirror on his truck.

"You're right, Logan, this doesn't look very confident, and to tell you the truth, I sure don't feel very confident. I actually feel pretty weak standing like this."

"You mean that having a weak posture actually makes you feel weaker?" Logan asked.

"You try it and tell me. I want you to do the same thing I'm doing so you feel it for yourself."

Logan put his head down and let his shoulders fall forward as he looked down at the ground. "Like this, Uncle Joe?"

"Tilt your shoulders forward a little more, hang your head, and now slouch your back like I am," Joe said, motioning toward his back.

Logan copied Joe's posture.

"So, how does that feel?"

"Not very strong, that's for sure," Logan replied.

"Go ahead and look in the mirror and see what it looks like. Do you feel confident with this posture?" Joe asked.

"No, not at all."

"Why not?"

"I'm not sure how to explain it. It just doesn't feel very strong."

"Do you feel weak and defeated?"

"That's it," Logan agreed again. "I feel weak, and I also feel bad about myself. Is that weird?"

"No, it's not weird at all. Your body language, especially the way you're standing right now, can have a direct impact on how you feel and how others see you. So, do you enjoy standing like that?"

"No, not at all."

"Then why are you standing that way?" Joe asked jokingly.

Logan looked up at Joe to see if he was joking, and when Logan's eyes met Joe's smile, he said, "Because you told me to."

They smiled at each other and laughed.

"So, let me get this straight. You didn't like standing in that weak, defeated posture?" Joe asked.

"No, not at all," Logan answered.

"Then, I want you to remember what that posture feels like and how it makes you feel inside. I also want you to remember that when you stand like that, or walk around that way, you're pretty much telling everyone that you're weak, defeated, and an easy target. It screams weakness and self-pity, and if you get in a habit of doing this, you'll start doing it without even knowing it."

Logan nodded his head yes, realizing that he often stood with his head down, avoiding eye contact. He told himself how weak that must look to others and decided that he didn't want to look like that anymore.

"Now I want you to try this: stand tall and pull your

shoulders back. I want you to lift your head up and look me directly in the eyes."

Logan did what he was told. He pulled his shoulders back, lifted his head up, and stood tall. But his eyes were still looking down toward the ground.

"Eyes here, Logan. Look right here," Joe said as he pointed to his own eyes and leaned in closely to Logan.

Logan lifted his eyes and locked in on Uncle Joe's eyes.

"Wow! Now that's impressive. Nice job, Logan. You look very confident!"

Logan smiled but then looked away and back down at the ground.

"Good job, Logan, but where are your eyes supposed to be?"

Logan raised his head, making eye contact with Joe.

"Very good! Now, keep looking here." Joe pointed to his own eyes again to make sure Logan stayed focused. "Good. So, how does that make you feel?"

"Pretty strong!" Logan said, looking at Joe's eyes.

"Great, now I want you to do the opposite again. I want you to put your head down and let your shoulders fall forward and just slouch."

Logan did what he was told.

"Now, show me how to stand confidently," Joe instructed.

Logan lifted his head, pulled his shoulders back, and made eye contact with Joe.

Joe nodded his head, signaling that Logan got it. "Now

that's communicating that you are strong and confident. I want you to remember how good this posture feels and how confident you feel when you stand like this. And don't forget to make eye contact." Joe pointed to his own eyes to make sure Logan didn't forget this key detail.

Logan continued to do his best, but old habits can be tough to change, so Logan dropped his eyes again.

"Back up here, Logan." Joe redirected Logan's eyes again. "I want you to remember that when you feel confident and you look confident, then you will speak more confidently. It's truly amazing how this all works together, and I can guarantee you that it works every time."

Logan nodded his head in agreement.

"Okay, Logan, let's move on to your lion's voice. Here's an example of how to use your lion's voice to tell a bully to leave you alone. It also works if you're being a hero for someone else who is being bullied."

Logan looked away from the mirror to watch Joe and saw how confident he appeared with his posture, his head, and most notably, his eyes.

"You need to stand tall with your shoulders back and head up, and you must make good eye contact. Even without saying a word," Uncle Joe continued, "you're showing that you're serious, and when you speak, speak clearly, calmly, and get directly to the point. Tell the bully 'Enough' or 'Stop it' in a firm tone that tells them you're serious."

"I've asked Doug and David to stop, but it doesn't do any good," Logan said, still holding on to the belief that nothing would ever stop them.

"As I said before, we may be well beyond this step with Doug and David since they've been bullying you for so long. We may need to do more to stop it. But your strong posture and confident tiger's eyes and courageous lion's roar will definitely tell them that you aren't playing around anymore, and it's time for this to stop."

"What does a courageous lion's roar sound like?" Logan asked.

Joe instantly got into a strong posture. His eyes seemed to burn a hole right through Logan and, without warning, he yelled out with a big booming voice, "ENOUGH!!!"

Logan was not only startled, but he was also truly scared and took a couple of steps back.

"Whoa ... that scared me," Logan said, shaking his head in surprise.

Joe raised his eyebrows. "That's my lion's voice," he said with a grin.

CHAPTER 10

AFTER LUNCH, they went back outside and picked up where they had left off. Joe had hung an old mirror in the back of the barn early that morning and took Logan over to it.

"All right, Logan. Now it's your turn. I want you to practice by looking in the mirror. I want you to show me your strong posture and your tiger's eyes. Then practice your lion's voice by saying 'Enough' loudly enough to convince yourself that it will stop a bully."

Logan looked in the mirror, rolled his shoulders back, and did his best to look intensely into his own eyes. But it didn't work. He just wasn't convincing himself. One thing was for sure: if he couldn't convince himself, he wouldn't be able to convince Doug and David.

Logan looked away from the mirror and, with his head down, asked, "Do you think I'll ever have the confidence to stand up to them?"

"Let's find out. Look at the mirror and envision Doug and David staring at you, just like they were at the hardware store, and then let that fear sink in."

"What?" Logan said.

"Look at the mirror and pretend Doug and David are staring directly at you. I want you to feel the fear that you felt yesterday at the hardware store."

Logan tried to do what Uncle Joe suggested but kept dropping his eyes and looking down at the ground.

"Fight through it, Logan. I know it's tough, but this is a huge turning point. Look in the mirror and envision Doug and David looking directly at you. You need to do this."

Logan tried to do it again. Even though it was much tougher than he thought, he was determined to do it.

He took a deep breath, lifted his eyes, and stared directly into the mirror. Within seconds, the fear he had experienced at the hardware store was all over his face.

Joe knew this would be painful for Logan. He also knew this was the only way for Logan to really dig deep inside himself to apply his best attitude and effort into his tiger's eyes and lion's voice. Sometimes, to find out how truly strong you are on the inside, you have to feel the pain as if it were real.

Logan broke eye contact with the mirror and instinctively assumed a defeated posture.

"Lift your head up! Now roll your shoulders back and show me your tiger's eyes!" Joe demanded. The power in Joe's voice actually scared Logan, and he immediately did what he was told.

"Now, look in the mirror and show me your tiger's eyes," Joe commanded.

Logan did it without hesitation. Surprisingly, he was standing straight with an intense look in his eyes. He had discovered his tiger's eyes. He wasn't exactly sure how it had happened, maybe it was the sound of Joe's voice combined with the pain he was feeling inside, but he felt strong, and the look in his eyes was intense.

"Now, feel all the pain that Doug and David have caused you. Let it burn inside you. Do you feel it?"

Logan nodded his head without taking his eyes off the mirror. His body began to shake a little as he felt the fear and then the adrenaline rush.

"Good. Now use the pain to release your lion's voice and yell 'ENOUGH!!!'" Joe yelled with the same loud, booming voice that caused Logan to jump again, but Logan never broke his focus. He was still staring intently into the mirror.

"Say it, Logan, and say it with your lion's voice. 'ENOUGH!!!'" Joe yelled out again.

"Enough," Logan said in a quiet voice.

"ENOUGH!!!" Joe yelled again.

"Enough!" Logan said, a little bit louder this time.

"Remember, Logan, I need your best attitude and your best effort in everything you do, especially this."

Logan nodded his head and kept looking directly into the mirror. He was locked in with his tiger's eyes on full display, but he still needed to find his lion's voice.

"I know how painful it is for you to think about what has happened, but it's that pain that's going to push you to use your lion's voice and dig deep enough to develop the confidence you need to make that pain stop. Now, look in that mirror and look deep into your eyes with the intensity of a tiger. Now yell at the top of your lungs with the power of a lion."

Logan was shaking all over as he again felt the pain from all the years of being bullied. He looked into the mirror with a look he didn't know he had, and then without hesitation, yelled, "ENOUGH, ENOUGH, ENOOOOUUUUGH!!!"

Hearing all the yelling, Molly walked outside to see what was happening.

No one said anything for a few seconds, and then Logan, who appeared to have been in a trance, snapped out of it. With sweat running down his face, he looked at Joe. "How was that?" he asked with a trembling voice.

"That was awesome. That's finding your tiger's eyes and your lion's voice," Joe said and held out his hand for a high five.

"WOW! That was intense. You really scared me," Molly said as she walked over and gave Logan a hug and a kiss on the cheek.

"Thanks, Mom," Logan said, hugging her back.

"So, how do you feel?" Joe asked.

Logan was still shaking quite a bit as he wiped the sweat from his face and answered, "Pretty good. It almost didn't seem like it was me."

Joe's pride was apparent. "That was awesome. Now you need to remember how you did it so you can do it anytime you need to."

"Okay," Logan said, starting to calm down.

"Since we're already in the barn, let's see if we're tougher than a bale of hay," Joe said as he walked into the corner of the barn.

Tougher than a hay bale? Logan thought while jogging to keep up with his uncle.

Joe grabbed a long rope, tied it around a hay bale, and handed the other end of the rope to Logan. "Can you do me a favor, Logan? Carry this rope up to the rafters and throw it around that rafter." Joe pointed to the rafter directly above them.

Logan climbed up the hay bales and threw the rope over the rafters before heading back down. Joe grabbed the end of the rope and pulled it so the hay bale was hanging in the air a few feet off the ground, then tied the rope to one of the horse stalls.

"Do you know what this is?" Joe asked as he pushed the hay bale.

"It looks like a punching bag," Logan replied.

"Yes, it does, and that's one of the things we're going to use it for. But the most important thing we're going to use it for is self-defense."

"Okay," Logan said with a puzzled look on his face.

"Are you ready?" Joe asked.

"Ready for what?"

Just then, Joe gently pushed the hay bale at Logan. Logan was slow to respond, and the hay bale bumped into him.

"Hey!" Logan yelled out, "I wasn't ready!"

"What?" Joe said, pushing the hay bale at Logan again.

This time, Logan put his hands up and stopped it.

"Good," Joe said as he pushed the hay bale back at Logan. This time, he pushed it with some extra force.

Logan put his hands up again, but the extra force knocked him back a step. He was a little stunned but didn't say a word.

"Let me show you something. Push the hay bale at me," Joe said as he took Logan's place directly in front of the hay bale.

Logan pushed the hay bale at Joe. Joe avoided it by stepping to the side and out of the way.

"Now push it at me again. I mean really push it, with some force."

Logan pushed the hay bale with much more force. Joe again avoided it by simply stepping out of the way.

Joe moved even closer to the bale to where he could touch it without extending his arm.

"Push it again and push it with all your strength. I want you to knock me over with it," Joe commanded.

Logan stepped back and ran at the hay bale. With a huge grunt, he pushed it with everything he had. And just like before, Joe simply moved out of the way, and the hay bale went swinging on by.

"Do you see what I'm doing?" Joe asked.

"Yes, you're moving out of the way," Logan replied.

"That's right! Do you think you can do that?"

"I think so," Logan said but with a lot of hesitation in his voice.

"Good, here it comes," said Joe, surprising Logan by how quickly he pushed the hay bale at him.

Logan barely got his hands up, but the hay bale still hit him squarely in the chest, nearly knocking him over.

"Dang it!" Logan said, clearly getting frustrated.

Joe pushed the bale at Logan again, and once again, the bale hit Logan square in the chest.

"Dang it!" Logan yelled out again but much louder this time.

"Are you getting frustrated?" Joe asked.

"Yes!" Logan yelled out.

"Is it helping you?"

"I don't understand," Logan replied in a frustrated tone.

"Is your frustration helping? Is it keeping you from getting hit?" Joe calmly asked.

"No," Logan said as he put his head down.

"Then what good is it to get frustrated?"

"I don't know," Logan said with his head still down.

"That's a lesson in itself. It doesn't do any good to get frustrated; as a matter of fact, it only makes things worse because when you're frustrated, your mind isn't thinking clearly. And, if your mind isn't thinking clearly, then you're not going to make the right choices," Joe said as he walked over and lifted Logan's head for him. "Remember, eyes up, no defeated postures."

"Okay," Logan said, holding his head up on his own, still sounding frustrated.

"Do this, Logan. Take a slow, deep breath, breathe air in your nose and out your mouth, and I want you to say the words 'Air in my nose, air out my mouth' in your head as you breathe."

Logan practiced this slow breathing while Joe repeated five times, 'Air in my nose, air out my mouth.'

When they finished the fifth time, Joe asked, "How do you feel now?"

"Better ... more relaxed," Logan said calmly.

"Are you still frustrated?" Joe asked.

"No, not really, I kind of forgot about it."

"Good, that's the second part of the lesson."

Logan looked at Joe with the same confused look.

"Logan, do you understand what just happened?"

"I think so."

"Then explain it to me," Joe replied.

Logan thought for a few seconds. "The breathing helped me relax, and I forgot about being frustrated."

"Very good. Now, do you think you can avoid getting hit by the hay bale?"

"I think so," Logan said timidly.

And just as the words were coming out of Logan's mouth, Joe pushed the hay bale at him. Logan tried to move out of the way, but he still got hit in the side.

"Man, I thought I had it that time," Logan said in an angry tone.

"Do you want me to show you how I avoid getting hit?" Joe asked.

"Yes, please!" Logan answered with a bit of frustration returning to his voice.

"Shove it at me again and really pay attention to my hands."

Logan shoved the hay bale and then watched as Joe effortlessly moved out of the way again.

"Okay, now shove it at me again, and this time, pay close attention to my footwork."

Logan shoved the hay bale at Joe again and then watched as Joe almost magically moved out of the way.

"Do you know what I did and how I did it?" Joe asked, looking directly at Logan.

"I think so. Didn't you just move out of the way?"

"Yes, that's part of it. Did you notice anything else?"

"Yeah, you didn't get hit."

"Sure, that's the result, but did you notice how I was standing and where my eyes and hands were each time?"

Logan shrugged his shoulders and looked down to the ground, struggling to find the answer.

"The answer is not down there," Joe said sharply. "Look here, Logan. This is your best defensive position. It's called a guard stance. You keep your hands open and out in front of you to create a barrier between you and the attacker. Keep your arms and legs about shoulder-distance apart and be sure to keep your tiger's eyes focused on the attacker. This is the first and most primary defense, avoidance, doing everything you can to avoid the attack and avoid getting hit."

Joe moved Logan's hands into the proper position and continued, "There are a number of reasons why you want to keep your hands open and out in front of you. When your hands are open, it shows everyone that you are trying to defuse the situation, keep the peace, and do everything to avoid getting into a fight. If you close your fists, it tells everyone watching that you're ready to fight."

Logan closed his hands into fists and then reopened them as Joe continued.

"Another reason you want to keep your hands open and your palms facing the attacker is that it's easier to keep your arms loose, which allows you to move much quicker. When you make a fist, your arms will automatically tighten up, making your arms feel heavier and your movements slower."

Next, Joe showed Logan where to hold his hands and how to cross his wrists to make an "X" with his arms directly in front of his body.

"This is my favorite defensive motion and the first one I teach to all my students. This technique is easy to remember and easy to do. Most importantly, it's very effective because it uses both arms to create a barrier between you and the attacker, and the angle of your arms will deflect the attack away. I call it an 'X' block."

Logan practiced the motion several times, being sure he didn't cover his face and block his vision.

"That really looks good, Logan. Now do that same thing with your hands, then turn your body to the side while stepping out of the way."

Logan practiced this at least a dozen times and said, "I think I've got it."

"You do?" Joe questioned, and without hesitation, he pushed the hay bale at Logan.

Bam! It hit Logan square in the chest again.

"Dang it!" Logan yelled out. He pushed the hay bale away in anger and stomped around in a circle, having a little fit, before realizing what he was doing.

Logan stopped and glanced over at Uncle Joe. Joe stood there, waiting for Logan to regain control. Logan paused, took a couple of deep breaths, and calmed himself down.

"All right, what happened?" Joe asked.

Logan looked down at the ground, shaking his head in defeat.

"Stop looking down there for the answer. Eyes up," Joe said as he pointed to his own eyes.

Logan looked up at Joe with a defeated look that said he just wanted to give up.

Joe, as if he were reading Logan's mind, said, "We're not going to give up. We're going to battle through this challenge, and that's what's going to give you the confidence to battle through the next challenge, and then the one after that. I believe in you, Logan, and you can do this. Now, tell me, where do you keep your eyes and your hands?"

"Up and forward," Logan replied.

"Very good. Now, are you ready this time?" Joe asked in a powerful tone. Before Logan had a chance to answer, Joe pushed the hay bale at him again. This time, Logan had his hands up and his eyes forward and was able to deflect the bale to the side.

"I got this!" Logan said, pumping his hands in the air.

Joe and Logan kept working on this one basic defensive technique. Over and over, Joe would remind Logan to keep his hands up and his eyes forward, as he repeatedly pushed the hay bale at Logan.

To challenge Logan even more, Joe had him stand closer and closer to the hay bale as he pushed it at him. This gave Logan less time to think and less time to get out of the way. His reaction time got faster and faster as he got really good at this drill.

"Are you feeling pretty good with this and ready for the next lesson?" Uncle Joe asked.

"Sure," Logan answered.

"Good. Then let's see how you do against a real attacker," Joe said, and without hesitation, he came running at Logan as if he were going to run him over.

Logan didn't move as Uncle Joe ran and picked him up like he was going to tackle him to the ground.

Logan's eyes were big, and he was obviously panicked.

"What happened?" Joe asked.

"I ... I ... didn't know you were going to run at me."

"So, it's a little different when it's an actual person running at you?" Joe asked.

"Yes!" Logan said as he nodded his head.

"Well, we're going to continue working at it until it's ingrained in your mind. The hay bale is a great way to practice, but to make it as real as possible, I want you to envision this hay bale as a real person running at you. Every time you practice, make sure you do it exactly the way I've taught you so that it becomes automatic and you can do it without thought. Repeat after me and memorize this saying: 'How you practice is how you perform.'"

"How you practice is how you perform," Logan repeated as they continued to practice this one technique. They would work with the hay bale for a while, and then Joe would run at Logan and try to tackle him.

Logan was getting better and better with his footwork and hand positioning, and his confidence was growing.

Joe wanted to make sure Logan really had it down, so he continued to pressure him by running faster and really trying to tackle him to the ground. He even started yelling and swinging his arms around like a crazy person, trying to scare and distract Logan, hoping to break his concentration and get him to freeze up. Instead, Logan kept his tiger's eyes locked in on Joe, maintained his strong defensive posture, and did the "X" block and sidestep motion every time.

Molly had walked out to the barn and had been watching for several minutes before Logan noticed her.

"Hey, Mom," he called, "check this out. Look what I've learned."

Joe pushed the hay bale at Logan. Just when it looked like it was going to crash into him, and just as Molly started to yell out, Logan calmly turned his body and stepped out of the way as the bale went swinging on by.

"Did you see that, Mom? What do you think about that?" Logan asked excitedly.

"WOW! That is impressive, Logan." Molly was truly impressed.

"OH YEAH!" Joe yelled as he ran at Logan, attempting to tackle him. This startled Logan for a second, and he started to freeze up, but without thinking about it, he put his hands up and did an "X" block while turning his body and stepping out of the way at the last second. He did the technique so well that he actually deflected Joe's hands to the side, causing Joe to be off-balance and crash directly into the hay bale.

"Wow! Are you okay, Uncle Joe?" Logan said as he ran over to Joe.

"Okay, are you asking me if I'm okay? Are you kidding me? I'm doing great. That was AWESOME!" Joe said as he picked up Logan and gave him a huge hug.

Molly came over and joined in the hug. She felt a tear of joy roll down her face as they all savored the moment, realizing that Logan's confidence was growing and that he was another step closer to becoming bully proof.

Later that evening, after replacing all the old boards and hinges, the three of them worked together to repaint the barn door the bright red color that Logan picked out.

Exhausted, they all slept peacefully after the successes of the day and felt excited about the next day's adventures.

CHAPTER 11

LOGAN WAS UP EARLIER THAN NORMAL and headed directly out to the barn to begin working on his defensive drills. He stood in front of the hanging hay bale and started doing his sidestep motions. Joe, who was just getting back from his morning run, stood at a distance, proudly watching Logan practice.

"Looking good, Logan. Your footwork is really looking good," Joe said as he walked into the barn.

"Thank you, Uncle Joe."

"Okay, now that you've learned the ABCs, it's time to move on to the 'D.'"

"What's the 'D' stand for?" Logan asked excitedly.

"The 'D' stands for defending yourself with physical force if necessary. This is an absolute last resort, and you must do everything you can to keep from getting to this step. However, there are times when it may be unavoidable, and that's why I'm teaching it to you."

Logan looked at Joe and nodded his head slowly as Joe continued, "If you really think about it, you're actually defending yourself with every step of the ABCs. The 'A' is being aware of the bully and trying to avoid the conflict. The 'B' is believing in yourself with your bully proof armor to block out the negative comments and actions. The 'C' is communicating clearly with your tiger's eyes and lion's voice to stop the bully without getting physical. And, the last drill we worked on, the sidestep and 'X' block defense, is a combination of all the ABCs but in reverse order."

"They are?" Logan asked, looking confused.

"Sure, they are. Think about it. You tried to communicate clearly with your tiger's eyes and lion's voice and your strong defensive posture, along with keeping your hands open, trying to bring peace. That's communicating clearly that you don't want to fight. Next, you believed in yourself with your bully proof armor by standing in your strong defensive posture. You were aware when the bully ran toward you, and you stepped out of the way to avoid the attack. So realistically, you've done absolutely everything in your power to avoid having to get physical."

"Wow," Logan said thoughtfully.

"However, sometimes there is no way to avoid physically defending yourself, and one of those times is if someone attempts to physically hurt you. This is called assault, and if they put their hands on you in a threatening manner, that is called battery. If this happens, they are no longer just bullying you; they have now committed a crime. By law, if someone assaults you, you have the right to physically defend yourself with enough force to stop the attack."

Logan listened as Joe continued.

"The most common attacks, especially at your age, are someone pushing you, or trying to tackle you to the ground, or swinging a wild haymaker punch at you. The best defense for these types of attacks is what we just worked on, the 'X' block and the sidestep defense. If the attacker continues coming after you, you will eventually have to do something to stop them. That's what we're going to work on now."

Logan's eyes lit up at the thought of learning something that would actually stop Doug and David.

Joe pointed to his hand and showed Logan where the palm heel of the hand is. Then he showed Logan where the solar plexus is located, just above the stomach, about a hand's width up from the belly button.

Joe lightly pushed his palm heel into Logan's solar plexus to show him how perfectly the open-hand palm strike fits into the solar plexus, almost like a key in a lock. He wanted Logan to feel how easy it is to get the air knocked out of him.

"The goal is to be as accurate as possible and to deliver the hardest palm strike you can to knock the wind out of the attacker, and then be ready to repeat the motion if necessary. When done correctly, this one technique will be all you need to stop the attacker right in their tracks. Once they've had the wind knocked out of them, it's very difficult for them to move or continue attacking you. The good news is this technique doesn't do much physical harm or have any lasting side effects, but it does hurt, and it's extremely effective."

Logan nodded his head, saying, "It is painful, and embarrassing. I remember one time when I was talking to a girl and David ran up and punched me in the stomach. It hurt so bad that I fell to the floor and couldn't breathe. I just lay there gasping for air as everyone laughed at me."

Joe shook his head, sympathizing with Logan. "That's why I call it the most effective, non-lethal technique."

"So, how do I do a palm strike?" Logan asked as he rubbed the palm of his hand.

"I'm going to teach you, but I want to be clear that you only do this if you are being physically attacked, and you have no other way to stop the attacker. Then, once the attacker is no longer a threat, you must stop. You are never allowed to hit a defenseless person. I don't care what they've done to you in the past, you must stay in control. If you continue to hit them when they're down and defenseless, you are committing a crime by using excessive force. Does that make sense?"

Logan nodded his head yes.

"A saying I've always liked is: 'We learn to physically defend ourselves, so hopefully we'll never have to.'" Joe walked over to the shelf, grabbed a pair of work gloves, and handed them to Logan.

"What are these for?" Logan asked.

"You'll see, just go ahead and put them on."

Logan slipped the gloves on as Joe walked over to the hanging hay bale.

"Do you think you can bust this hay bale apart?" Joe asked.

"Do you mean by punching it?"

"No, with a palm strike," Joe replied. And then without saying another word, Joe did a massive palm strike to the hay bale. It seemed to explode from the twine and fall to the ground in pieces.

"Wow!" Logan said, amazed at what he had just seen.

Joe grinned. "That's a palm strike."

"Can I try it?" Logan asked.

"Absolutely, but first we need to get another hay bale down," Joe said, pointing to the empty rope that just seconds earlier was holding a hay bale.

Logan quickly grabbed another hay bale, lugged it over to Joe, and the two of them hung it up just like the first one, which was now scattered all over on the ground.

As soon as the bale was in place, Logan began hitting it with his palm. Not much happened. The hay bale just swung back and forth as he continued hitting it.

Logan glanced over at Joe and saw that Joe wasn't wearing any gloves, so Logan took his gloves off. He hit the hay bale and discovered that it didn't feel very good on his bare hand, so he put the gloves back on and tried again.

After several more minutes, Logan put his hands up and asked, "Okay, how'd you do that? How did you knock that hay bale into pieces with just one hit?"

"Many, many years of practice," Joe said, smiling.

"Can you teach me how you did it?" Logan said as he took off his gloves and wiped his sweaty forehead with the back of his hand. Joe patted Logan on the shoulder. "As I promised, I'll show you everything I can, but it is up to you to listen, learn, and do your very ..." Joe paused, waiting for Logan to finish the statement.

"BEST!" Logan yelled out.

"That's right, your very best, and do you remember what happens when you put forth your very best?"

"When I put forth my very best, I'll become my very best," Logan confidently said.

"That's right, and if you don't ..."

"Then I won't."

"You're awesome, Logan!" Joe said as he put his fist out for a knuckle pound.

"Thank you," Logan replied cheerfully and went back to hitting the hay bale. His power was increasing, and his self-confidence was growing.

Joe continued working with him to help increase his power. He reminded Logan to use his whole body, not just his arm, when delivering the strike. He gave the example of hitting a home run in baseball and how there's a huge difference between just swinging with your arms and using your entire body.

The two of them practiced this one motion over and over with both the left and right sides. Logan struggled at first with his left hand, but he knew that giving up wasn't an option, so he dug deeper inside himself and battled through.

After hitting the hay bale for another fifteen minutes, they stopped and grabbed a drink of water.

"Do you think I'll be able to do what you did?" Logan asked.

"What, break a hay bale?" Joe replied.

Logan nodded his head as he took another sip of water.

"Absolutely!" Joe said convincingly. "It will just take some time and dedicated practice, but I know you can do it as long as you continue to have the right attitude and effort."

Joe took another big drink of water, and then without warning, he squirted water on Logan from his sports bottle.

"Hey ..." Logan said as the water splashed on him.

The two of them were playing like little kids, running around the yard, laughing and throwing water all over each other.

Molly watched them playing through the kitchen window. It was obvious that Uncle Joe was exactly what Logan needed, not only the lessons on how to become bully proof, but also the fun-loving father figure that he missed so much.

After drying off and getting cleaned up, Joe and Logan had a huge bowl of strawberries with whipped cream and then headed back outside to enjoy the day and continue their "D" lesson on defending yourself.

As Logan leaned against the porch railings, his thoughts were interrupted when Joe said, "There's an old saying, 'When you go around looking for a fight, you'll surely find one.' You might think that getting into fights makes you tougher, and a lot of people are mistaken about that, but really it just feeds the bully inside yourself."

"Sort of like feeding the bad wolf," Logan blurted out.

"That's exactly right." Joe continued, "A terrible result of being bullied is that it often leads to anger management and emotional issues that cause the victim to want to lash out and fight at even the smallest things."

Just then, Logan's cat, Patches, walked up, weaving between Logan's feet, wanting attention.

"There's the perfect example of fighting versus defending," Joe said, squatting down and rubbing Patches's neck. "Think about it. Patches doesn't go around looking for a fight; she just minds her own business and lives her life. But, if she ever felt threatened and was forced to defend herself, she would use the ABCs to become bully proof."

"Wait ... what? You think Patches knows the ABCs?" Logan laughed.

Joe chuckled. "Actually yes, I do. The truth is I created the ABCs to become bully proof based on sweet, innocent little kitty cats like Patches, and their primal instincts to defend themselves."

Logan reached down and rubbed Patches's back as

she sprawled out on the porch, basking in the warmth of the sun.

"Imagine that Patches is just minding her own business like she's doing now, and you sneak up without warning and scare her. What's the first thing Patches is going to do?"

"She's going to jump up and run off," Logan answered.

"Yes, she is, and that's the 'A.' She became aware of you, and aware that you scared her, so she avoided conflict by getting away from you. She will remember that you scared her and will avoid being around you for a while."

Logan nodded in agreement as he continued to pet Patches.

"Now, if you keep bothering Patches, what's she going to do next?" Joe asked.

"Um ..." Logan mumbled, "I'm not sure," he finally said.

"She's going to do the 'B.' She's going to believe in herself and put on her bully proof armor to block out whatever you're saying or doing. Essentially, believing in her abilities to protect herself but still trying to avoid physical conflict. And then what happens if you keep bothering her? What's she going to do then?"

Logan thought a moment then said, "I think the hair on her back would stand up, and she would hiss at me."

"Yes, that's exactly right, and that's the 'C,' communicate clearly the best way she can with her defensive posture, tiger's eyes, and furious lion's voice, which for a cat is their scary hiss."

"That can be pretty scary!" Logan added.

"Yes, it can. And if you still haven't learned, and you continue to bother Patches, and if you back Patches into a corner and she feels physically threatened, then that sweet little innocent kitty cat will do everything she can to 'D,' defend herself. She will claw your face and bite you as many times as it takes to stop you from attacking her."

Molly joined them on the porch and sat down by Logan.

Logan continued to rub Patches's back and then looked over at Joe. "Did you get into a lot of fights, Uncle Joe? I mean, until you figured this out?"

"Let's just say I made a lot of mistakes when I was younger."

"Mistakes like what?"

"Well, I went from being bullied nearly every single day to fighting anyone who was rude or disrespectful to me."

"Oh, did you win every fight? Were you scared? Who taught you how to fight?"

"Slow down, Logan. I got into a lot of fights because I didn't know any better and I had a lot of pain and anger trapped inside."

"So who taught you how to fight?" Logan continued quizzing his uncle.

"Well, my dad taught me at first. His idea of defense was to hurt someone bad enough in a fight so everyone would be afraid. If everyone was afraid of me, no one would want to mess with me."

Logan looked surprised to hear this.

Joe noticed the look on Logan's face and responded,

"Your grandpa didn't know any better. He did the best he could with the knowledge and experience he had. That's just how he grew up. He thought he was helping me fix my bullying problems, and I will always love him and your grandma for doing everything they could to help me."

Joe paused and then continued, "Besides, they didn't know about most of the bullying I was going through because I tried to hide it from them, which wasn't a smart thing to do."

Joe could see the look in Logan's eyes, and he knew that Logan could relate to this.

"Trying to hide this from my parents only made things worse. Because if you get into a habit of hiding things from your parents, before you know it, you're hiding everything from them, which is a recipe for disaster."

"I can see that," Logan nodded.

"That's good if you can learn that at your age because being a teenager, you may tend to think that you have all the answers to life's problems and forget that your mom has a little more knowledge and life experience. Plus, she's always there to help."

Logan nodded his head, showing he understood. "I know she is," he said, then asked, "Was your dad proud of you for fighting back?"

Joe paused and let out a long exhale before answering, "My dad wasn't around much when I was younger. It wasn't his fault; he was always working, trying to provide us with everything he never had. But I do remember one time when

I was about your age and I got in a serious fight. A kid had been bullying me for a long time, and I never did anything to stop it. When I finally had enough, all the built-up anger came out, and I completely lost control of myself."

"What happened?" Logan asked.

"Well, this kid, Eric, would kick me in the legs or smack me across the face and even kick me in the groin sometimes and then run away. One day after this happened, I came in crying, and my dad stopped me and yelled at me. He told me that the only way Eric was ever going to stop was if I hit him back and made him stop. Well, a couple of days later, Eric was at it again. At first, I didn't do anything. I just stood there as he kicked me. Then I heard my dad's voice in my head, and the next thing I remember was my mom screaming and yelling as she was pulling me off Eric. Apparently, I tackled Eric to the ground and got on top of him and repeatedly hit him in the face. There was blood everywhere, all over my clothes and all over him. I had broken his nose and split his lip. It was a very scary scene, and looking back, it really scared me because I was out of control."

"But he started it, and you were just doing what your dad told you to do," Logan replied.

"Sure, and that's exactly what I wanted to believe and exactly what I thought my dad would think."

Joe paused for a moment, unknowingly rubbing his chin while thinking back. "I remember getting in so much trouble with my mom, but all I could think of was how proud my dad was going to be. I had done exactly what he told me to do. I hit Eric back, and now, I thought, he would never bully me again. To tell you the truth, I don't know that I've ever seen my mom so scared or so mad at me, but I just blew it off because I knew my dad was going to be proud of me."

"Was he?" Logan asked.

Joe shook his head side to side. "No, he wasn't, and to my surprise, when he got home, he was furious. He yelled at me, asking what I thought I was doing beating this kid up. He wasn't happy. I tried to explain what happened, but he didn't want to hear it. He just kept yelling at me, asking if I thought I was a tough guy and if I was going to pay this kid's medical bills. I was so confused because I thought that's what my dad wanted. I thought he wanted me to fight back, to be a tough guy, just like him. But I was wrong."

"Why was it wrong?" Logan asked.

"It was wrong because I had turned into the bully, and I went far beyond just defending myself. I lost control and continued to hit a defenseless kid. You see, that's the huge difference between defending yourself with enough force to stop the attack, and fighting out of control. I know now that this happened because I had so much pain and anger built up from never defending myself that when I finally did, I lost control."

"I feel like that sometimes. I just feel so mad that I could explode, and it scares me. I guess I hold it all in, but the pain and anger just make me feel bad about myself," Logan said as he looked down to the ground and then back up to see Joe's reaction.

"It can certainly do that, and that's exactly why I am teaching you everything and why I'm having you work so hard in the barn. The physical workout is a great, safe release of all that anger, too."

"I do feel better after hitting the hay bale," Logan agreed.

"Good, I'm glad it's working. You are gaining the courage and confidence that took me over thirty years to develop and, most importantly, becoming bully proof at a young age so that you have the confidence to overcome any fear that you have and the wisdom to battle through every challenge you face. I want you to become the hero you were born to be, and most importantly, I want you to live your best Kickin'Life."

After several seconds, Logan looked at Joe and said, "Thank you, Uncle Joe, I'm really happy you're here, and I'm very thankful you're helping me. I don't want to hurt anyone, and I don't want to get in trouble. I just want the bullying to stop."

"I am truly thankful too," Molly said as she got up from her porch swing, walking behind Joe to give him a big hug around the neck.

"I'm glad I'm here, too, and I'm going to stay as long as it takes."

Logan smiled and found a spark of hope in himself that

he hadn't had before. "Yes, I will, I will become bully proof! And what's a Kickin'Life?"

Joe's smile couldn't have been any bigger. He was hearing the growing confidence in Logan's voice, and he answered, "Yes you will, Logan! I am so proud of you and the young man you are and the man you'll be. Kickin'Life is a phrase I use that means living your best possible life. It means you're kicking life's butt by getting back up and standing tall every time life or a bully tries to knock you down. You display the courage and confidence to believe in yourself and believe in your God-given talents to be who you were born to be, to stand out in the crowd, and to stand up to any bully you face, both real and in your mind, to live the life you were born to live. That's a Kickin'Life!"

Logan could feel the energy and power coming from Joe, motivating him to get up. "Let's get back to work, Uncle Joe. I'm ready to become bully proof and live my best Kickin'Life."

Joe jumped up and headed to the barn, where they spent the rest of the day reviewing the defensive techniques and learning some cool martial arts moves.

Joe showed Logan a few sparring combinations and some punching and kicking techniques that would help Logan with his coordination and balance, along with developing his speed and power.

Logan learned just how powerful he was and how much damage he could actually do if he lost control of himself. It reminded him to focus on only defending himself and not to take a chance of losing control and fighting. They worked on the proper placement of his hands and feet to ensure that Logan was doing the techniques correctly from the start.

Joe reminded Logan about the power of habits and how hard bad habits are to live with and how difficult they are to break. "They're like digging up weeds in the garden," he said. "It's best if the weeds are never allowed to grow."

Logan remembered that the 'weeds in the garden' example was one of the first lessons Joe taught him. It was also the one he referred to most often. Logan was starting to understand just how important it is to keep the weeds out of his mind's garden.

After dinner, Molly, Joe, and Logan played cards while Logan shared the ABCs to become bully proof with his mom. He held up his index finger to signal the first step. "The 'A' is awareness to avoid conflict. I need to be aware of everything going on around me, and then do everything I can to avoid conflict."

Then he held up a second finger. "The 'B' stands for believing in myself. I have to put on my bully proof armor so I can block out the negative arrows and be confident in my abilities to defend myself."

Logan held up a third finger then tilted his head to the side and thought for a few seconds before continuing. "The 'C' stands for communicate clearly. I get into a defensive posture and communicate to the bully with my tiger's eyes and lion's voice that I've had enough. And, if that doesn't work, I go and clearly communicate to a teacher or coach and explain to them exactly what happened."

Logan paused and glanced over at Joe to make sure he got them right.

Joe nodded his head, signaling for Logan to continue. Molly felt relief as she listened to her son confidently and courageously explain the ABCs to become bully proof.

"And, if A, B, or C don't stop the bully, or if they put their hands on me, then it is no longer just bullying, it's a crime. Uncle Joe said that if someone commits a crime against my body, then I have the right to physically protect myself."

"Agreed. So what do you do?" Molly asked.

"Well, I tell them to stop with my tiger's eyes and lion's voice. If they touch me or try to throw a punch at me, then I defend myself, and if they don't stop, then I do a palm strike," Logan said as he demonstrated an "X" block and then a palm strike.

"That's exactly right, Logan, now tell your mom what area you hit with the palm strike."

"I do a palm strike directly to the solar plexus." This time, Logan pointed to his solar plexus. "This is the area just below the ribs that knocks the air out of you," Logan said as he poked his solar plexus with his fingers.

Logan continued, "Uncle Joe said that if I do it right, this one technique will be all I need to stop the bully. And it really does hurt. David hit me there once, and I couldn't breathe."

Logan paused, then surprising his mom, he quickly

lifted his head up, rolled his shoulders back, and stuck his chest out like a superhero, saying, "But that's not going to happen again!"

Joe looked down at his arms as he felt goose bumps roll up them, and proudly said, "YES, Logan, YES! That's the attitude, that's the confidence, that's the hero I'm talking about."

Molly got up from the table and gave Logan a really big hug. "I love you so much, Logan. I'm so proud of everything you're learning." Logan had Molly stand up so he could show her again how to execute a powerful palm strike.

"I think I'm going to take you with me during my next speech and let you explain the ABCs to the crowd. That was perfectly said," Joe added, reflecting on Logan's huge breakthrough moment. Logan was able to reflect on a painful memory of being bullied, but instead of putting his head down in defeat, as he'd done so many times, he showed confidence and belief in himself. In that moment, Logan had moved well beyond "just hoping that things would get better" to "things are better, and the best is yet to come."

CHAPTER 12

IT WAS RAINING THE NEXT MORNING when Joe woke up. This was the kind of day that made him want to hit the snooze, but he had read a quote years ago that stuck with him: "Excuses are the nails that built the house of failure." He thought of it whenever he felt tempted to make an excuse or to try and justify breaking a good habit.

Joe had been staying with Molly and Logan for nearly two weeks. Next weekend, Logan was returning to his hockey team and would inevitably face Doug and David. Joe had decided that today he was really going to push Logan to the next level and a step closer to becoming bully proof.

The rain had stopped, leaving a chill in the air as they started the morning chores. When the chores were done, Logan hopped up to the rafters and did ten pull-ups and then twenty pushups in between a couple of hay bales.

Joe then had Logan lie on the ground as he put a hay bale on top of his stomach. He taught Logan how to get out from under the hay bale and on top to get the better position.

This was very tough at first, but Logan kept fighting and didn't give up, and after a couple of tries, he was able to roll the hay bale over and end up on top of it.

"Okay. Good job. Now do a palm strike in the area where the solar plexus would be," Joe said, pointing to the hay bale.

Logan gave the hay bale a pretty good palm strike.

"Do you think that really would've stopped the attacker and knocked the wind out of someone much bigger than you?" Joe asked.

"No, probably not," Logan replied.

"I don't think so either. Remember, how you practice is how you perform. Let's do it again."

Logan did the palm strike again, and this time, he yelled "STOP!" as he hit the bale.

Joe nodded his head to show his appreciation. "Much better! Now let's do it from the start," Joe said, putting the hay bale on top of Logan again. He held the hay bale to keep it on top of Logan, forcing him to really fight to get it off.

Logan struggled at first and then started getting frustrated, and at one point, looked as if he was about to give up. "Don't you give up, Logan! Don't you do it! Come on! Keep fighting! Work at it! Push it off! YOU CAN DO IT!" Uncle Joe shouted encouragingly.

Logan continued to struggle while Joe continued to apply pressure on the hay bale, raising his voice with encouragement.

"I'm not letting you give up. You've got to push me off. YOU CAN DO IT! COME ON, LOGAN!"

Logan kept struggling but dug deep and found strength he didn't know he had. With one huge shove, he yelled out, "GET OFF OF ME!" as he pushed up so hard, it knocked Joe off-balance. Logan immediately rolled on top of the hay bale and delivered the hardest palm strike he'd ever done while yelling at the top of his lungs, "STOP IT!"

Logan's heart was pounding, and the look in his eyes showed Joe everything he'd wanted to see. Logan had found his inner confidence.

"WOW! Now that's what I'm talking about," Joe said as he helped Logan up and gave him a huge high five.

"I didn't think I could do it," Logan said, shaking from the rush of adrenaline.

"Well, you did do it, and I mean, you really did it. I didn't let up and neither did you. You dug deep inside yourself and battled through. Great job!"

After they grabbed a quick drink, Logan repeated a question he'd been wondering about. "Uncle Joe, who taught you all of this?"

"Well, I've learned a lot over the years from a variety of influences. The one who taught me the most about self-defense was one of my first and favorite instructors who I met on a military base. He was a little rough around the edges, so to speak, and you never would've guessed he was a master at martial arts and a self-defense expert, but his knowledge and understanding of personal protection is the most influential part of the self-defense that I practice and teach today."

Joe thought back on all his years of intense training. He smiled, knowing that his instructor would be very proud of the work he'd been doing over the past several decades, and especially today with Logan.

"He was really good?" Logan asked.

"He was better than good. He had a rare quality about him. He was a very gentle, kind man on the inside, but his large frame commanded attention, and his knowledge of self-defense was second to none."

Logan was visualizing the man as he asked, "Do you still see him?"

"From time to time, but just like with you, I'm going to do a better job of making time, because life's too short not to."

Logan smiled at the thought of seeing his Uncle Joe more often.

They worked hard, hitting the hay bale with a variety of punching and kicking combos, then they reviewed the "X" block and sidestepping defense. Logan kept trying to bust up the hay bale the way Joe did with a palm strike.

"Are you tired?" Joe asked when they paused and grabbed another drink of water.

"I'm exhausted," Logan replied, wiping the sweat from his forehead.

"Good. Let's see what you're really made of." Joe climbed up onto the hay bales, jumped up on the rafters, and did twenty pull-ups.

"Your turn," Joe said, looking down from the rafters.

"I don't know how many I can do. My arms are sore."

"I think you can do ten," Joe replied with confidence.

Logan jumped up on the rafters, did five pull-ups and then hopped down. "That's all I've got. I'm too tired," Logan said, rubbing his arms.

"No excuses, Logan! You only did five pull-ups because you convinced yourself that you were too tired to do any more. Do you remember what I said about avoiding negative self-talk?"

"But ..."

"No buts, this is an important lesson about battling through your challenges, overcoming adversity, and not giving up on yourself. I know we've worked hard today, but I believe in you, and I believe you can do more. You didn't give up when you were wrestling the hay bale, and I'm not going to let you give up with this either."

Logan knew this was true.

"This is about your attitude and effort, and I'm going to make sure you have the right attitude and effort before next Saturday when you walk back into that locker room and see Doug and David."

Logan nodded his head as Joe continued. "Remember, the right attitude is the fuel that drives you to put forth your best effort."

Logan could feel his heart beating faster as Joe's words pumped him up.

"Logan, you are a lean, mean, muscular machine," Joe said in a loud, confident voice.

"Say it with me. 'I am a lean, mean, muscular machine!'" Joe yelled out.

"I am a lean, mean, muscular machine!" Logan said as he flexed his biceps.

"That's it!" Joe said as he pumped his fist in the air.

"Say it louder!"

"I'm a lean, mean, muscular machine," Logan said much louder.

"Say, 'I CAN, and I WILL!!!'" Joe shouted loudly.

The power in Joe's voice nearly lifted Logan up onto the rafters by itself.

"I CAN and I WILL!" Logan yelled out.

Joe looked directly into Logan's eyes and said, "You must get used to pushing yourself beyond what you think you can do. You must always believe you can do more than what you've done, especially when you're tired. Now say, I AM going to do ten pull-ups."

"I am doing ten pull-ups," Logan replied.

"I am strong enough!" Joe yelled.

"I am strong enough!" Logan repeated.

"I am good enough!" Joe yelled out.

"I am good enough!" Logan shouted.

"I can do this!"

"I can do this!"

"I will do this!"

"I will do this!"

"I am going to do this!"

"I am going to do this!"

"I will not give up!"

"I will not give up!" Logan was shouting.

"I BELIEVE IN ME!"

"I BELIEVE IN ME!"

"I CAN, I WILL, I AM!"

"I CAN, I WILL, I AM!" Logan was screaming by now.

Joe's voice got louder with each command, and so did Logan's.

"Now get your butt up there and knock out those ten pull-ups!" Joe commanded.

"Yes, sir!" Logan said, and without even thinking, he jumped up to the rafters and in seconds, he had done ten pull-ups. Just as he was about to hop down, Joe yelled, "Do another one!"

Logan struggled but did another one.

"Do another one!" Joe said again.

Logan struggled again but pulled himself up one more time.

"And another."

Logan did what he was told and did another pull-up.

"One more."

"But ..."

"No buts, do another one!" Joe commanded.

Logan, sweating, struggling, and grunting, did one more.

"Last one, Logan, you can do it. One more, Logan, I believe in you."

Logan grunted and groaned and yelled at the top of his lungs, "YES!!!" as he pulled his chin above the rafter beam for the fifteenth pull-up.

"You did it, Logan, I am so proud of you. You didn't think you could do ten pull-ups, and you ended up doing fifteen," Joe said as he helped Logan down so he wouldn't fall.

Logan plopped down on the hay bale next to Joe.

"So, how do you feel?" Joe asked, smiling ear to ear.

"Tired!" Logan said with sweat dripping off his face.

"I'm sure you are, but how do you feel inside? How do you feel in your mind?"

"I feel awesome!" Logan grinned.

"That's because you are awesome."

"Thanks," Logan said, still trying to catch his breath.

"You are very welcome, Logan."

"Do you think I'll ever have enough power to knock the hay bale out of the ropes like you did?"

"Yes, I do. As long as you keep practicing and working hard and doing your best, then yes, it will happen," Joe said with enough confidence to convince anyone who was listening.

They walked by the hay bale, and Logan said, "HI YAH!!!" as he hit it again. The hay bale swung back and forth but didn't break apart.

"Nice technique and great power, Logan. You're getting close, buddy, keep at it," Joe said as he gave him a thumbs-up.

Throughout the week, Logan was pushed well beyond what he believed he could do. Joe pushed him to do more pull-ups, more pushups, and more sit-ups. He pushed him to carry heavier buckets of water and fuller wheelbarrow loads, and he pushed Logan to get quicker and quicker with the defensive attacks and maximize his power with the palm strike. It was clear that Logan had made a great transformation in just a few weeks, but Joe knew that the added boost of confidence from knocking the hay bale apart would be the thing to bring it all together. Joe wasn't going to do it for him, nor was he going to loosen up the bale. Logan was going to have to do it on his own, just like he was going to have to face Doug and David on his own, and that day was coming soon.

CHAPTER 13

IT WAS FRIDAY NIGHT. Christmas had come and gone, and school was starting back next week. Soon, Logan would return to the ice rink and play in his first hockey game after a few weeks off. It also meant that he was going to see Doug and David.

He had accomplished so much in the time with his Uncle Joe. They had fixed the barn door and repaired several of the horse stalls, they had cleaned the barn and weeded the garden, and most importantly, they had rebuilt Logan's confidence to a level it had never been before. They all knew the real test was coming up very soon.

As they were finishing up their last night of training, Joe had Logan work on the palm strike attack again and again because he was determined to help Logan break the hay bale into pieces.

Logan was getting tired, and as much as he wanted to break up the hay bale, he also wanted to make sure he was well-rested for the game tomorrow.

Joe walked over, put his arm around Logan, and gave him a hug. "I'm so proud of you, Logan. You've impressed me so much over these past several weeks. Let's head in and get a good night's sleep. You've got a big day tomorrow."

The next morning, Joe let Logan sleep in a bit, knowing his body needed the extra rest. Joe took care of all the morning chores after his normal morning workout and was sitting outside on the porch when Logan walked out.

"So, what do you say we go bust up that hay bale?" Joe asked.

"I was hoping you'd say that." Logan smiled.

When they got to the barn, Logan warmed up and worked on his defenses before hitting the hay bale.

"Okay, are you ready to break this hay bale?" Joe asked in a firm tone.

"Yes, I am!" Logan replied with confidence.

"Then hit!" Joe commanded.

Logan hit it hard, but nothing happened.

Joe raised his voice, saying, "Hit it again with everything you've got."

Logan hit it again, much harder this time, and to his surprise, he could see a small section of the bale fall to the ground.

"HIT IT AGAIN, HARDER!" Joe yelled out.

Logan hit it again, and a little more fell from the ropes.

"HARDER!" Joe yelled out.

Logan hit it again, and a little more fell from the ropes.

"GIVE IT EVERYTHING YOU'VE GOT!"

Logan paused, took a breath, and hit it again, even harder this time, and more hay fell from the ropes.

"YOU'VE GOT THIS, LOGAN—GIVE IT EVERYTHING YOU'VE GOT WITH YOUR LOUDEST YELL! YOU CAN DO THIS!" Joe yelled at Logan with encouragement.

Logan could feel the energy from Joe's words, and he let out his loudest yell. "HI YAAAAHHHH!!!" and hit the hay bale with everything he had.

It was a massive palm strike, and Logan felt his hand drive through the hay bale and out the back side. Hay particles flew all over him as the remainder of the hay fell from its ropes and crashed to the ground.

"I DID IT, I DID IT! Uncle Joe, I DID IT!!!" Logan yelled, jumping up and down and celebrating like he had just won a championship.

"Yes, you did, Logan, yes, you did!"

They both celebrated in the barn before running into the house to tell Molly about this huge accomplishment.

Logan couldn't stop talking about breaking the hay bale as he got ready for the game. He was excited to see his friends and get back on the ice. He was truly pumped, and even though he was a little nervous about seeing Doug and David, he was enjoying this feeling of invincibility. When they pulled into the ice rink parking lot, Logan took a deep breath and said, "Well, here goes."

"You've got this, buddy," Joe said, helping Logan get his equipment out of the back. "I'm proud of you, Logan."

"I love you, Logan. Have a great game and do your best." Molly gave Logan a hug. "We'll be in the stands, cheering you on!"

Logan turned and walked toward the front door of the ice rink.

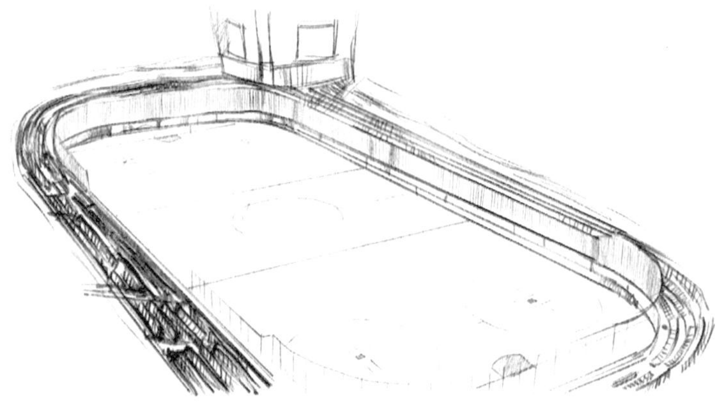

He could feel panic and fear set in. It had been almost a month since the severe bullying caused him to nearly quit the sport he loved. Since then, he had trained nearly every day with his Uncle Joe. He had learned more about himself than he had his entire life.

Logan knew he could defend himself against a bale of hay in the barn. Now, as he was walking back into the ice rink, back to the place that used to bring him so much joy, he just hoped he could do what he needed to do to stop the bullying once and for all.

He reached the main entrance, and his hands started to shake as all those old feelings of fear came back. He took a deep breath. Even though every single part of him wanted to turn around and head back to his mom's car, he remembered Uncle Joe's words: "*Logan, I've given you all the tools, I've shown you how to use them, now it's up to you to do what you need to do ... no one can do it for you; you have to do it for yourself. I believe in you, your mom believes in you, but in the end, you must believe in yourself.*"

Logan took another deep breath and blew it out, then opened the door and walked in.

As he walked through the lobby, a few parents said hello and a few others welcomed him back. He could feel his body continue shaking as he headed to the locker room, but he kept going. As his hand reached for the locker room door, he heard Doug and David's voices yelling obscenities at another kid.

A part of him had hoped they wouldn't be there, but they were, and he was about to face them. He took a slow deep breath in through his nose and then out his mouth and thought to himself *no turning back now*. He opened the door.

Instantly, all eyes turned to him. Noah, Ethan, and a few other players came up and high fived him and said, "Welcome back, Logan, we missed you." He smiled. It was good to be missed and even better to be greeted by his buddies.

When Doug and David shifted their insults and obscenities toward him, the good feeling disappeared.

Logan took a breath, looked directly at them, and calmly said, "What's up, boys?"

This caught Doug and David off guard. They weren't expecting Logan to say anything at all, and they certainly weren't expecting the confident look in his eyes.

There was a brief pause, and just as Doug and David started to say something, Coach Jacobs walked in and made his way over to Logan.

"Logan, I'm so glad to see you, welcome back, we've all missed you."

Doug and David mumbled something under their breath, but everyone just ignored them.

As the team finished getting ready, Coach Jacobs went over the lineups and game plan. Logan was happy that Coach Jacobs was in the locker room, and he was glad to hear that his line would be starting the game. Logan hadn't played in over a month, and he was really excited to get back on the ice and play the game he loved. He was nervous at the start of the game, but it went away when he scored a goal on his first shift.

It was a hard-fought game and a great team effort, and Logan ended up scoring two goals, including the game-winner late in the third period.

After the game, the players walked into the locker room, celebrating their 4–3 victory. Doug and David were already there waiting; they had gotten kicked out of the game in the third period for a cheap shot on a smaller player and then for arguing with the referee.

"Wow, I can't believe you losers won a game without us," Doug yelled when the rest of the team walked in.

Everyone ignored them and kept celebrating their hard-fought victory.

"I guess the crybaby actually did something to help the team ... that's a first," David said directly to Logan.

"Yeah, instead of crying," Doug said in a hateful tone

Logan and the rest of the team continued ignoring them. Coach Jacobs was quick to come into the locker room and congratulate the team and remind them of practice in the morning, and then he was gone.

As the players began changing out of their equipment into their regular clothes, Doug and David started in on Logan.

Now is the time to put the ABCs to become bully proof to the test, Logan thought.

He took a breath and did what he could to 'A'void and ignore their insults, even when Doug demanded that Logan look at him so he could see if Logan was crying. Logan continued ignoring them, even when David got in Logan's face and began screaming at him as he finished getting dressed.

As fewer and fewer players were left in the locker room, and as Logan got up to leave, Doug grabbed his shoulder and said, "You gonna cry for me tonight, little baby?"

Logan, believing in himself, pulled away from Doug, and with his tiger's eyes and lion's voice, yelled out, "DON'T TOUCH ME!"

Surprised by Logan's voice, Doug stepped back.

Logan turned and walked out the door, but he didn't take his eyes off the two of them.

Doug and David looked at each other, surprised that Logan had actually said something back to them, especially considering that a week ago, they had bullied him at the hardware store and he had just stood there in fear.

"So, you think you're a tough guy now?" Doug asked as he and David got up and ran out of the locker room after him.

Doug tried to grab Logan and drag him back into the locker room, but Logan deflected Doug's hand away with the outside-inside defense he had learned from Joe.

"I SAID DON'T TOUCH ME!" Logan yelled out in a confident tone.

Logan continued walking toward the lobby, when suddenly Doug came charging at him.

Logan moved out of the way just like he'd been trained to do, and Doug ran right by him.

David, standing by and watching, began yelling and taunting Logan, screaming, "You're going to get it now, tough guy."

Now they were in the waiting area, just in front of the lobby, so there were a handful of players from both teams walking by, and the excitement caused a crowd of kids to gather around.

David and Doug continued taunting Logan, and just like before, no one said a word or did anything to stop it.

Logan was on his own again, but he no longer felt helpless. His confidence was soaring after he had successfully deflected and avoided the first couple of attacks, and for some reason, their words weren't really affecting him. He truly felt like he was wearing bully proof armor, and all their insults were just bouncing off. He saw something he'd never seen before: he could see self-doubt in Doug's eyes as he stood there looking at him.

Then Logan, with his tiger's eyes and lion's voice, said, "Enough, and I mean it."

Doug and David looked at each other in total surprise at what they were seeing. Logan wasn't backing down. The look in his eyes was a little intimidating, and his voice actually sounded confident. But they were in too deep now to stop. Several kids had gathered around, and there was no way they were going to let Logan show them up.

Molly and Joe were walking to the lobby with the rest of the parents when they heard yelling and chanting from a group of kids who had formed a large circle.

Molly's stomach felt like it hit the floor as she looked directly at Joe. "Do you think Logan is okay?"

"Let's go see," Joe answered calmly.

Molly's heart raced as she hurried over just in time to see Doug run at Logan in an attempt to knock him to the floor.

Logan calmly, but with a speed and quickness that surprised everyone, sidestepped and deflected Doug's attack, knocking Doug to the floor.

Doug landed hard on the concrete floor and lay there for a second in disbelief. David, not believing what he had just seen, came running at Logan, yelling like a wild man. As he closed in on Logan, he lowered his shoulder to try and tackle him to the floor, but Logan did what he was trained to do in the barn; he visualized the bale of hay swinging at him, and he stepped to the side, avoiding David's attack. David, surprised that Logan was able to get out of the way, quickly turned around and ran at Logan again, but this time, he threw a wild punch at Logan's face.

Just then, Molly yelled "LOGAN!!!"

Logan briefly lost focus and looked toward his mom. As he turned back, he was able to get his hands up and turn to the side, deflecting most of the punch. David's fist still connected with Logan's cheek, causing instant pain. Logan's cheek was burning from the punch, but he wasn't fazed and immediately got in his guard stance as David threw two more wild punches. Logan blocked both punches with the "X" block, and just as David wound up to throw another punch, Molly yelled, "DO THE PALM STRIKE!"

Logan quickly and powerfully did a palm strike to David's solar plexus, stopping him immediately. David fell to the floor, holding his stomach and rolling around in pain.

Doug, seeing that Logan's back was turned, ran up and grabbed him from behind and tried to throw him to the ground. Logan, again, did what he had been trained to do and spun around to break the grip while delivering a hard palm strike to Doug's solar plexus. Doug instantly fell to the floor next to his cousin, holding his stomach and trying to catch his breath.

Logan walked over to them and yelled, "ENOUGH!!! Don't ever touch me again!"

This fight was over. They weren't getting up, and they weren't going to attack Logan again. He had successfully defended himself, and he was able to stay under control, even after getting hit in the face and even after all the years of bullying.

But just because this fight with Doug and David was over didn't mean that everything was over.

Molly had frantically worked her way through the crowd, and as she reached Logan, Bob slammed into her, nearly knocking her down. He and Mike were pushing and shoving their way over to their sons, who were lying on the floor.

Bob and Mike were furious because, in their minds, their boys were making them look bad.

Bob immediately started yelling at his son, "Get up and do something, Doug. Don't just lie there."

"Don't be a pansy. Get your butt up and teach him a lesson," Mike growled at David.

The other parents just stood there, not saying or doing anything, just as they had always done. It was Logan and Molly in the middle, and everyone else standing around too terrified to help out.

Mike suddenly turned toward Logan. "So, you think you're a tough guy with that karate crap your uncle taught you?"

"Yeah, where is your uncle, the karate sissy?" Bob said, trying to intimidate Logan.

Molly turned and stepped in front of Logan, shielding him from Bob and Mike.

"I'm right here," Joe said as he stepped forward.

Molly turned to Joe, and even though she was shaking, said, "I got this. There's something I want to say to them."

Joe smiled and nodded his head as he backed up a few steps to give Molly some room. Joe was actually hoping Molly would take charge and prove to all the parents watching that any bully, regardless of the size or how long it had been going on, can be defeated by simply standing up to them.

Mike snickered at Molly, telling her she better get out of the way or she might get hurt. Molly stood her ground. "Enough is enough! Everyone in this town has had enough of your bullying!"

Bob, who wasn't about to be talked down to, grabbed Molly by the shoulder and pushed her to the side, saying, "Women ..." in an extremely derogatory tone.

Joe took a step forward, but before he got another step, Molly regained her balance and immediately turned back to Bob and delivered a powerful palm strike right to his solar plexus, sending him crashing to the floor, holding his stomach and gasping for air.

"DON'T YOU EVER TOUCH ME!!!" Molly yelled out at Bob, and then turned and looked Mike directly in the eyes, showing him her tiger's eyes.

Mike looked at Molly and started to say something, but before he got a word out, Molly yelled out with her lion's voice, "YOU WANT TO JOIN HIM?!"

Mike paused, looked to the floor, shook his head, and turned and slowly walked away.

Everyone in the crowd breathed a sigh of relief and began clapping as they made their way over to Molly and Logan. Molly couldn't believe what just happened, and neither could anyone else. Several of the parents apologized to Molly for not helping her and Logan, and several of the dads, including Coach Jacobs, walked up to Logan and told him how proud they were of him.

The players gathered around Logan with excitement. "How did you learn to do that karate stuff?" they asked, talking on top of each other. "Can you teach us how to do it?"

Logan grinned. His confidence was stronger than it had ever been. He had defeated his archnemeses, Doug and David, and he had done it in front of all his teammates at the ice rink, one of his favorite places. Plus, his mom, whom he'd taught the palm strike, showed the entire town how to stand up and defeat a bully who's much bigger than you.

Joe had stepped out of the crowd and positioned himself where he could clearly see Bob and Mike, and their boys, to make sure they weren't going to try anything else. He wanted Logan and Molly to enjoy their moment.

That night in bed, Logan had a hard time falling asleep. He was excited about everything that had happened at the ice rink, but he was also sad that Uncle Joe was leaving.

CHAPTER 14

THE NEXT MORNING, Molly, Logan, and Joe drove to the same restaurant where it had all begun just a few short weeks ago. Molly rode by herself, and Logan rode with Joe, in his truck.

Logan talked the entire trip to the restaurant. He was still excited about what had happened the night before and about everything he had learned over the past three weeks.

As Joe flipped on his left blinker to turn into the restaurant, Logan stopped talking. He knew that Joe was leaving after breakfast, and it felt like he was losing his best friend.

They had worked together nearly every day over the past three weeks, and for the first time in his life, he finally had a best friend and someone to fill the void of missing his dad.

"You okay over there?" Joe asked as he put the truck in park and glanced at Logan.

"Yeah ... I'm good," Logan said, trying not to sound sad.

"It's okay, buddy, I'm going to miss you too." Joe reached over and messed up Logan's hair.

"Thank you for everything, Uncle Joe," Logan said as a tear rolled down his cheek.

Joe nodded his head and smiled. "You are so welcome, Logan, and thank you for being such an amazing young man and an incredible student."

Joe saw Molly's car pull into the parking lot, and when she saw Joe's truck, she pulled in next to it.

"Hey boys," Molly said as she got out of the car.

"Hey Mom," Logan replied.

"Hey Molly," Joe echoed.

"Well, who's ready for some breakfast to start the day?" Joe asked as he clapped his hands together.

Logan and Molly both nodded.

During breakfast, they talked about all the amazing things that had happened. They seemed to talk forever, and time appeared to stand still as they reflected on everything from the first day that Logan saw Joe walking across the parking lot, to the training in the barn, to last night at the ice rink, and now at their last breakfast together.

They got quiet when the server brought them their receipt and thanked them for coming in. The three of them looked at each other and then got up and headed for the door. As they walked out to the parking lot, they tried to think of how to say goodbye.

Molly paused as she remembered how depressed Logan

was and how scared she was before she reached out to her brother for help. She remembered how reluctant she was to call Joe because of all his fighting in the past. But now she was overwhelmed with pure joy as she hugged him goodbye.

"I am so very grateful, Joe, for everything you have done for us. I can't thank you enough."

Logan joined in on the family hug. He remembered how close he had been to giving up on life, and how all that had changed when he first saw his Uncle Joe walking across the parking lot at this very restaurant. He felt like a completely different person. So much had changed in such a short period of time, and so many thoughts were racing through his head.

As they ended their group hug, Logan was holding back tears. "Thank you so much, Uncle Joe, for everything. I will never forget you. I wish you didn't have to go."

"Never forget me? I'm not going away forever; you can get ahold of me anytime you want. As a matter of fact, I've enjoyed being back in town so much that as soon as I get a few things in order, I'm going to move back here so I can keep a closer eye on you."

"Are you serious? That would be awesome!" Logan excitedly replied.

"I am, and I'm just as excited as you are. I am the lucky one here who got a chance to know such an amazing young man, and I'm not going to let that go. Just think, a few weeks ago, you had very little confidence in yourself, and you had a difficult time even making eye contact with me.

Now look at you: you're back on the hockey team, scoring goals, winning games, and dealing with bullies."

Molly and Logan smiled as Joe continued.

"I am so blessed to be your uncle. I love you, and I have loved spending time with you. I know there were times when you wanted to give up and quit, and I know there were many times when you didn't fully understand the lessons I was teaching you, but you never gave up. Because of that perseverance, you are now bully proof. You've gained the greatest strength anyone could ever possess,—self-respect."

Logan smiled and tried to hold back the tears that were streaming down his face. These tears were the opposite of the tears that he had shed a month ago when he was ready to quit hockey and give up on life; these were tears of joy, appreciation, and success.

"I want you to keep practicing everything I showed you, and when I get back here, I'd love for you to help me share the ABCs to become bully proof with as many kids and adults as we can. The more we talk about being bully proof, and the more knowledge we pass on, the greater the impact we are going to have on society. And if we're able to help just one person get through a rough season of their life, just think how much of an impact that will make. Little by little, one by one, we can make a difference, and that's the first step to living a Kickin'Life."

"That would be awesome! YES! I'd love to help. Did you hear that, Mom? Uncle Joe wants me to help, isn't that great?" Logan was almost unable to contain his excitement.

Molly proudly agreed that Logan would be the perfect person to share his experiences to help others.

"Well, I guess my work here is done," Joe said as he gave Logan and Molly one more big hug then turned and got in his truck. "I'm proud of you, Logan, and I can't wait to see you again in a few months."

Logan and Molly thanked Joe again, and as he drove away, Molly turned to Logan and said, "I love you, Logan."

"I love you, too, Mom. Now, let's get an early start living that Kickin'Life."

THE END

MORE PRAISE FOR *BECOMING BULLY PROOF*

"Becoming Bully Proof will help you know exactly how to live your life free from the onslaught of others who would do you harm."

—Chris Widener, *New York Times* and *Wall Street Journal* bestselling author, international speaker and Member of the Motivational Speakers Hall of Fame. —*The Art of Influence*

"...not only is this a story written for kids who are dealing with bullies in their daily lives, it is also written for the 'kids' in all of us who continue to live with the ramifications of times when we didn't defend ourselves with the right words, the right actions, or strong boundaries to keep our now adult hearts safe and protected."

—Kristen L Schindler, Author of *All the Things*, Podcast Host of "All the T.H.I.N.G.S with Kristen Schindler"

"Rich Grogan's years of expertise have finally come together in this easy-to-read, family-style book with "hands-on" instruction, as well as the mindset needed to overcome the ever-growing problem of bullying."

—Grandmaster Karen Eden, author and instructor, 7th Dan, Tang Soo Do.

"Becoming Bully Proof is a very unique perspective on meeting your younger self and what you would do to help them get through the troubling parts of life ... It makes you think what you would tell your younger self and who were the influences that got you through those times."

—Master George Manns, 8th Degree Black Belt (Soo Bahk Do Moo Duk Kwan)

"What Master Grogan has done is taken something that we have all encountered at some level in our life and put it into a relatable and transformative story. As my son and I read this together, we found ourselves rooting for Logan and learning how to become bullyproof ourselves. This is a must read. The examples from the book are as easy as ABC and sometimes D."

—Jamie Morgan, Clinical Director and Counselor at My Family Counseling and author *Master of Circumstance*

"Becoming Bully Proof is a fascinating revelation...an intricately detailed narrative of how bullying happens and how to peacefully and confidently confront and overcome it."

—Laurie Magers, executive assistant to Zig and Tom Ziglar

"Rich Grogan has written a must-read book for anyone looking to defeat the bullies in their life! Read this book and learn from one of the best!"

—Rick Marteeny, president of Rick Marteeny Insurance Agency, Inc.

"The secret is out. Master Rich Grogan is no longer a hidden gem in a small Midwestern town karate studio. His principles and ideals have shaped the members of our community for years. This book merely scratches the surface of who Rich Grogan is. Under his disarming smile and weathered patina lies a man who can and will affect positive change in this country. Pay attention, and you will see it too."

—Jimmy and Stacy Jesse, Entrepreneurs
in Edwardsville, Illinois

"GREAT BOOK!!! I highly recommend it to everybody! It's empowering in a way I never knew existed and you will be better after reading it – I promise!"

– Cindy Ziglar Oates, Ziglar Inc.

ABOUT THE AUTHOR

MASTER RICH GROGAN, creator of the Grogan's Bully Proof System and best-selling author of *Becoming Bully Proof*, is on a mission to empower 10 million people with hope, faith & confidence to believe in themselves to stand up to every bully they face, both real & in their minds.

Master Grogan is passionate about bringing his unique, uplifting messages to audiences around the world because nothing is more vulnerable than someone who doesn't believe in themselves.

His experience with bullying as a child, parent, martial arts instructor and physical educator led him to understand that being able to defend oneself against bullying works from the inside-out, and is as easy as ABC.

Master Grogan is a 6th Degree Black Belt with over 40 years martial arts experience.

He has worked with kids for more than 35 years, coaching sports, teaching physical education in public schools and instructing martial arts. In addition he's the host of the Grogan's Bully Proof Podcast, a certified Ziglar Speaker & Life Coach, and the founder of Grogan's Martial Arts, one of the largest martial arts academies in the Midwest. He is a Christian, father of three and loving husband.

He would love the opportunity to empower your family, team or business with the hope and confidence to believe in themselves to stand out in the crowd and become bully proof.

To learn more about hiring Master Grogan as a speaker,
or to buy his book visit his website:
www.warriorconfidence.com.

CONNECT & FOLLOW

Follow on Social Media for free content
& daily bully proof inspiration:

Facebook, Instagram, You-Tube, Tik Tok:
@realrichgrogan

Email: rg@warriorconfidence.com

For more information about Master Rich Grogan, to join his life changing bully proof program, and to buy his books or bully proof apparel, or to hire him to speak at your next event, visit his websites:

Website:
www.warriorconfidence.com

MORE BULLY PROOF

Available in paperback
amazon.com

www.ingramcontent.com/pod-product-compliance
Lightning Source LLC
LaVergne TN
LVHW090935080826
845145LV00003B/751